Manilla felt her breasts rise, nipples harden . . .
The other women pressed back, her softness moving,
moving against the denim of Manilla's jacket and
jeans.

The waves of heat eased, then rebuilt, moving her
closer to the brick wall behind them. Manilla's palms
were suddenly against the rough red facade of the
building, pressed there for balance. Her brain rebelled
at the intrusion, aghast at this forced dance, even as
her body responded.

Behind them the street moved like a river. They
were simply two dark stones at the water's edge. The
current eddied and parted around them.

The woman held her knee between Manilla's legs,
forcing them wider apart. Moving rhythmically now,
the motion matching the growing heat, the pulse. The
blood rose in Manilla, pounding at the temples; she
was swollen, wet, open — against her will, but ready,
ready for this stranger . . . a stranger, who, only
moments before, had struck her, raising blood . . .
And now . . . now . . . where was Ginny?

Virago

KAREN MARIE CHRISTA MINNS

The Naiad Press, Inc.
1990

Printed in the United States of America
First Edition

Edited by Katherine V. Forrest
Cover design by Pat Tong and Bonnie Liss
   (Phoenix Graphics)
Typeset by Sandi Stancil

Library of Congress Cataloging-in-Publication Data

Minns, Karen Marie Christa, 1956—
   Virago / by Karen Marie Christa Minns.
      p.   cm.
   ISBN 0-941483-56-8
   I. Title.
PS3563.I4735V57   1990
813'.54--dc20   89-48970
                                                          CIP

For Jayne,
my intriguer

ACKNOWLEDGEMENTS

To Bruce Bennett, Barbara Dickinson and Katharyn Machan Aal; my mentors, my honest friends . . . and to Katherine V. Forrest, novelist, for unending patience and holy sisterhood. You are pagan god(dess) parents to this book.

SPECIAL THANKS

To Darrell for Sunday copy service; Trish for a spare typewriter; Helen C. and Diane V. — this is a thank-you note from long ago; to Marcia and Canelake for the love.

PROLOGUE

". . . 3. hag, beldam(e), Jezebel, jade, nag, shrew, fishwife; murderess; ogress, harpy, Fury, maenad; adulteress, paramour, mistress; prostitute, whore, harlot, strumpet, trull, trollop, wanton, loose woman, courtesan, madam(e), procuress, bawd, hussy, streetwalker, drab, white slave; dragon, harridan, vixen, virago . . .
4. monster, fiend, demon, devil, devil incarnate, fiend in human shape; Frankenstein's monster; cannibal, bloodsucker, vampire, ghoul, vulture, ogre . . ."

from The New American Roget's College Thesaurus in Dictionary Form, 1962

3

PART ONE

Paris, France . . . some time before . . .

The candle floated toward her as if some hand carried it. There was no hand. She closed her eyes. Final. The choice made. No ghosts here, only a dark angel; invisible but moving with the light . . .

The bed was soft, fresh linen pulled tight; the white an intense reminder that there was no return. Carefully she stretched out, feeling rather than seeing the approaching flame. Only moments left . . . final seconds in this present . . . the last pure heartdrum that she might honestly claim. After this act there would be no pulse, no steady dancing of her own veins. She was not sorry . . . only . . . a little afraid . . .

The candle lit down upon the night table. Suddenly, so swift it was that it took her breath from her, a hand touched her brow. Light; light as the flight of the fire from the middle of the mantle to her bedside; light as the air surrounding them. Honeysuckle, jasmine tea and tuberose, all mingling with the sacred smoke from the beeswax.

The hand (my God, so quick and gentle!) traced a perfect line across her brow. She wanted to laugh . . . nerves or an overriding sense of the Catholic presence . . . as if at any moment the high strains of Mass sounding from choir-boy throats would rise. A kind of atrocious sacrament then, so be it. She opened her eyes as the fear drifted away.

The older woman was very close. Her long dark hair trailed over her shoulders like honey. Her eyes were a jeweled blue, cold as the precious stones they so resembled. The lips were pale, fine, slightly drawn back. Only if you realized and knew where to look would you suspect the truth. She knew. Her only care was that soon, soon those quiet lips would part and reveal the miracle . . .

The older one hovered over her; fingers like hummingbirds traced nectar trails over her flesh. As they circled her aureoles the nipples leapt up eager, eager, even as the mind and otherflesh. She felt the dense, hollow pounding between her thighs; the great vein there carrying fire as well as its ruby flow. In its beat was the echo of her hunger. She called the older one's name, called her closer, called her to move quickly. She was burning with the want of it. She knew that this was what she had been born to — she knew and arched her back with the knowing.

Pressing her belly towards the older woman's face, feeling the exquisite tongue part her dressing gown and begin its hot descent, she breathed out the final

8

breaths of her life. Her hands began to caress and tangle themselves in the mane of dark hair — soft, softer than any she had ever touched, softer than her own. There were no sounds now save for the pulsepound and the wretched moan escaping from her own throat . . .

Sweat bathed her, made her mad with its tickle and salt burn. She could wait no longer, indeed, had waited a full twenty years for this act. She cupped the back of the older one's head and brought it down, down, down to those other, lower lips. She felt her moisture rise, her vulva heavy with ache that would not be stilled. Her heart seemed to have lowered itself and was now pumping its lifesong between her thighs.

Throbbing, her need making her open wider than she imagined she could be opened . . . There was a single movement that was more pain than pleasure as she felt those pale, soft-petalled lips of the older woman part her own, pull back and sink down into that most secret place . . . sharp, hot . . . It was then that she cried the older one's name . . .

PART TWO

Upstate New York . . . the present . . .

"Darsen . . . how does one get a name like that? Is it a family name?" The college woman stroked the outside of the sweating drink, lowering her eyes, the movement not in the least bit coy. Blatantly she followed the delicate lines from throat to breast where the black leather was slit, exposing a second skin. She liked what she saw. Unusual, it was very unusual to be attracted to someone her own age.

"A family name . . . yes." Darsen laughed softly. Her voice was musical like tubular wind-chimes, but only gently lilting. Darsen did not drop her own stare; she met the coed's with a flash of icy blue.

The young woman was momentarily stunned. A ripple of delight ran over her stomach, shivered along her veins. Slowly it descended, melting into a quiet burn. She felt the hunger call deep, deep. She uncrossed, then re-crossed her legs. Her bottom lip felt heavy and soft. Her eyes were half-lidded. Almost involuntarily she ran her tongue over her lips, tasting beer and the trace of Rocking Red Lipstick. Still the older woman stared.

"My name's . . . Gerry . . . Regina, actually . . . but that's so stuffy." She blinked hard, pulling back a bit, realizing she was almost brushing against Darsen. She sipped her drink. My God, when had anyone made her feel like this? Darsen wanted her, but it was more, she wanted Darsen. Oh yeah . . . Two years since she started "experimenting" with women . . . She was always the one in control . . . This was so different . . . More than any guy, this come on, strong, strong, but all Darsen had done was sit next to her at the bar. She'd simply asked the older woman her name — but why? She wasn't into "older women" . . . and the leather — please. Darsen was sheathed in it — even her hands! It was old enough to scare Rambo away. But she wasn't scared. Darsen's smile had melted her down to explosion.

"Regina's a beautiful name. I think you should keep it." Darsen's elegant hand stroked the edge of her own wine glass.

Regina was captivated by the slender fingertip at the edge of the crystal . . . the bloody liquid moving back and forth . . . the rhythm almost the same as the cunt thrump surrender Darsen reduced her to. She wanted to be the glass in Darsen's hand . . . Surely she was as wet . . .

"Maybe tonight I'll keep my name, for you, Darsen." There, she'd said it and saying it sealed something between them. Never before had she liked her christened name. She'd always felt as if it belonged painted on a boat. Tonight, however, rolling from Darsen's lips it sounded luscious, regal, like some secret they now shared. She found herself wanting a secret, close and dark, between them. She watched in shocked fascination as her hand reached out hypnotically and touched the sculpted cheek of Darsen. Soft, so soft. Cool — like flower petals in the night air. She didn't take her hand away even when she felt the blush burning her cheeks.

Darsen laughed again — that smooth, windswept sound. She covered Regina's fingers with her own black-gloved palm. She squeezed them firmly, declaring her intent and attention in the same press. She did not have to voice it. Regina's eyes were frozen, deadlocked with her own.

Loudly enough for two or three people close by, but not loudly enough to cause attention, Regina answered: "Yes."

The alley seethed with lake fog. Dense, scented with decaying leaves, wet stone, autumnal surrender, it mouthed them in.

Darsen's grip was firm on the wrist of the younger woman. Regina did not complain. She uttered no sound. Inside her head a long, slow scream was growing. It would not live, would not find its way out.

There was no one. If there had been it would only appear as if two slender college women were walking on together, clearing their heads before returning to Collegetown, back to their dorm. It would appear as if the older of the two was guiding a slightly tipsy sister around the lake shore, to sober her up. Tender, it would seem. Then, before the onlooker could break from the reverie, the fog would have swallowed them up.

But there were no onlookers as they left the alley and headed toward the beach. In the morning there would be a but a few scraps of torn cloth clinging like seaweed to the public dock . . . That and one set of footprints leading to the water . . . Regina's . . . Regina's alone.

"I'm not obsessing!" Manilla stood outside the shower.

"What? I can't hear you, I've got soap in my ears." Ginny's deep laugh broke the tension. No arguments, not tonight.

Manilla sighed. It seemed like anything could set her off these days. Okay, she had to be cooler. Ginny was still so damned sensitive about their arrangements. Hell, if anyone should worry, she should. Ginny had the Collegetown studio, she was the Cornell woman now. Ginny was . . . well, Ginny.

The water cut off. The shower curtain whipped back. A long tanned leg moved from behind the steamy plastic. Manilla caught her breath. Even after three years Ginny could still break her open with just a movement. So much . . . so much . . . why didn't Ginny trust that yet? Why didn't she know it, just know it deep like Manilla? Ginny was so unaware of her own beauty . . . Manilla reached out playfully toward the tight dancer's leg.

"Don't try it kid or we'll never make the opening!" Ginny moved out of the claw-footed tub onto the bath mat. Her tall frame glowed from the scalding shower. Her hair was plastered in honeyed tendrils to her face and back, deep gold against golden skin.

"Gin, let's skip the gallery." Manilla was embarrassed now as her hunger rose to the surface. Awkward, always too easy — maybe she should hold back more. Her friends told her that. But no, no way with Ginny. "Gin, I have to be back by midnight, you know the rules — why don't we just go out for dinner and come back here?"

"Manilla, this is David's first truly marvelous show in Ithaca — I promised! He's been so good to me — I'm committed. Wait, doesn't that sound awful — I mean, I want to go. Consider it penance for all the talk I've had to endure about your 'new advisor,'" Ginny smiled, pulling the towel away from her lover.

Suddenly, she moved in close. She pressed tightly against Manilla. So much intensity wrapped in such a small package — Ginny knew Manilla knew she was so much stronger than herself. Manilla was her protection. Like a force field, sometimes. When had anyone ever cared as much? Ginny depended on Manilla. Damn it — why did jealousy always make her act so crazy? Hearing about "the new advisor" all afternoon had set her off. Manilla never spoke of the faculty — she hated Weston — hated having another year there — hated that Ginny was thirty-six miles down the lake. Suddenly, to hear about this anthropologist, this most likely gorgeous, brilliant, older woman, well, it was like a glass of cold water in

17

her face. Ghosts rising. Oh, Manilla had been loyal from the start, but her reputation, the early years at Weston — Ginny had to push it behind her. One more year and Manilla would be out of that suffocating trap of a college. She could come to Cornell, move into Ginny's studio . . . If Ginny lost Manilla now, right along the edge of that final year . . . She pulled the small woman closer.

"Ginny, what? What?" Manilla pushed away a bit, bemused.

"Guess I'm feeling a little ragged tonight, sorry, it's been a long week." Ginny took a deep breath. Why were the simplest things the most vulnerable? It should be so easy, like home, like home was supposed to be — not this crystal shatterability. She looked down into Manilla's serious face, the dark eyes too deep for color. Ginny attempted a smile.

"I love *you*, Gin. I'm sorry I went on about Professor Slater. Poor timing on my motor-mouth, as usual. It's just that here she is, the first woman to head the department. You know how the art department palmed me off to old man Jones in anthro — he didn't want me, I didn't fit anywhere. Mix that with all the rumors and back-talking I have to put up with — well, she's like some kind of gift, you know? She thinks I'm serious enough about anthropology to be all right combining it with my art — and she's willing to take it on as a double-major. They probably just want to make it tough for her, too, Gin. You know how Weston is. Stupid slimy scrotums . . ."

"Manilla!" Ginny laughed, shaking out her hair, the momentary terror shut down.

"It's true. The stupid, tight-assed, sanctimonious

sexists are killing that school. They finally allow a woman on campus to run the department and they dump on her everything they don't want to handle — me included. Well, this time I lucked out. Anyway, she's probably old and tight-assed herself . . . she had to get the job somehow. She'll always be one of them, you know, 'the enemy,' the other side."

"Yeah, just your type!" Ginny grabbed Manilla's face and held it between her palms.

"Since when? Anyway, I only fly with dancers." Manilla pulled the towel from Ginny's breasts. She closed her eyes and pressed her lips to the warmed flesh. The hunger rose.

Ginny spread long fingers through her lover's curly hair, pulling the dear head closer, moaning softly as Manilla traced slow circles around her nipples. Yes, yes, they would definitely be late for the opening . . .

"Well, so glad you could make it. For a while there I had my doubts." Raising a knowing eyebrow, David hugged Ginny. A new wave band blasted in the next room, the scents of imported cheese, new paint and cheap chablis swirled around them, mixing with the music.

"This is great! Congratulations, David!" Manilla extended a gloved hand.

David's huge paw covered the small, black-clad one. "It means a lot to me that you're here, Manilla. I know what a royal pain it must be to escape from that girls' school." He winked.

"Women's college," Ginny corrected.

"Right," Manilla laughed, "a real sacrifice. Notice the bloodied brow?"

"Seriously, you don't have to run right off, do you?" David asked. "You are spending the night in town?"

"Well, actually, I was going to catch the last college van back in. I have a class that starts early tomorrow." Manilla felt her face redden. This was the real world, adults at a gallery opening, Ginny's world. She was still "the kid" tonight with a curfew . . . dammit. She didn't look at Ginny.

"Ahh, the salad days of youth . . . I remember my own very well. Anyway, dearhearts, you must scan 'The Work.' Drink, dance, later I'll pry your esteemed opinions from those pretty heads. Right now moi must mingle! Critics from the *Voice* just waltzed in and I'm negotiating a show in the Village. See you both later." David kissed Ginny's forehead and melted into the crowd.

"The Work": David's photographs were immense. Monster-scale car parts seemed like high-tech fossils from a flashy past, handsome as well as disturbing. Loud: everything in the gallery was very, very loud. Still, Manilla had to admit, she was glad to be there. Ginny was stunning in the backless cocktail dress, all black satin and long red gloves. Her dancer's body glided through the mass of people, attracting all eyes. Manilla felt fine. She wasn't as polished and was definitely the punk of the pair, but she was okay, attracting her own admirers. It would take a while, but she and Ginny were going to make it. They had written off the odds-setters a long time ago. They were very good — that good together.

Manilla touched the edge of Ginny's elbow, just

letting her know she was close and happy. Ginny spun around, suddenly smearing Manilla's cheek with a kiss. They laughed, toasting David, the art, each other. It had turned out to be a fine evening.

Across the gallery another woman looked on. As if she could see through the center of the crowd, she bore a hole straight towards Manilla and Ginny. When someone blocked her gaze she simply "moved" them. A frightening chill, a bit of panic, overwhelming and inexplicable, the targeted individual would simply move, conscious only of that fine shudder stretching from sole to spine.

The woman was taller than Ginny. She was no dancer, too slender and frail. Her hair was ebony and fell in a straight cascade down her back, thick and shimmering. Her black velvet gown revealed almost translucent skin. Ruby-tipped fingers were like five small wounds at her throat as they rested there, absently stroking.

For the briefest moment, Ginny turned, meeting the stranger's gaze. Blue tundra, frozen flame, a vast winter chill, held her. She paused mid-sentence.

"What, Ginny? Hey, you okay?" Manilla moved between the portly Cornell man and her lover. Ginny was colorless.

"Sorry . . . I feel strange . . . maybe the paté?" Her weak smile faded and she went down in a pool of black satin.

"David!"

He heard Manilla's panic over the roar of the band. As if in slow motion a group suddenly moved together in a tight circle, then back. David was mesmerized for a moment at the choreographed movement. By the time he reached them, Ginny was sitting up, her head tucked ungracefully between her legs. She was as pale as the weak chablis.

"Jesus, what happened?" He knelt beside Manilla, reaching for a glass of water someone held.

"She was fine, then she went white. Do you think it could be food poisoning?" the Cornell professor asked meekly.

"Really, I'm all right, I drank my wine too quickly and it's so hot in here . . . I'm fine." Ginny struggled to her feet but almost crashed a second time.

David caught her, moving her toward the gallery entrance. The air wafted in coolly, carrying the lake fog in its arms. Slowly Ginny's color returned. The air was like a soft palm at her temples, against her face.

The momentary break healed, the party resumed behind them. David let Ginny lean against him. Manilla stood close by. Her own skin felt prickly-strange, chilled.

"Okay sport, I'm calling a cab. Manilla, can you stay with her tonight? I'll be hard to reach if she's really ill . . ." David looked from the pale Ginny to the darker face of Manilla.

"Manilla's got to get back to Weston," Ginny protested.

"Fuck my first class!" Manilla took Ginny's arm, pressed it under her own.

"My sentiments exactly." David smiled.

"Baby, you miss too many classes and they'll take the grant away — they're just looking for an excuse," Ginny said.

"Sshh. The cab's here, someone must have called

from inside. Let's just take it back to the studio."
Manilla squeezed Ginny's hand.

"Ginny, she's right. Let her borrow your Bug
tomorrow to get back to campus and you can use my
car till the weekend. The important thing is making
sure you aren't alone. Now, be good you two!"

"No more cheap wine, I mean it." Ginny leaned
against the younger woman, grateful for Manilla's
familiar solidity. Manilla grounded her, as usual, as
always. This darkling, her changeling, her miracle —
how had her life been before they met? Like a rare
and polished stone suddenly washed up on the
volcanic beach, Manilla shone for Ginny. Just for
Ginny. Manilla was her true magic. Ginny leaned
against her, fighting the pounding behind her eyes.
She was never sick, never had headaches; no, it was
more than the wine. What? What? Like a fist around
her heart, just for a moment she could feel its
rhythm change, a strange but not painful pressure
. . . then it was gone. Oh God, what? She was a
dancer! If this meant something was wrong with her
heart . . . no! Not now, she couldn't think of that
now . . . it had to be the flu or the paté. Maybe she
needed vitamins. The year had already been strenuous
— it was going to be a long haul. She had to do it,
tough it out, for both of them. She could do it as
long as she wasn't alone . . . thank God . . . not
alone ever again. Some stupid virus wasn't going to
take it away . . .

* * * * *

23

In the gallery doorway a tall woman with icy eyes and long dark hair watched the taillights of the cab. She watched until the blood-colored points were lost, enveloped by the fog. Then she turned and went back inside.

The steps behind him were soft, registering only that someone smaller shared the fog-bound street. He lit an unfiltered Player and dragged the smoke deep into his lungs. As he inhaled, he noticed he could still smell the girl on his fingers. He grinned. Young — the way he liked them. Tender. Hey, it was a public service, right? She was a student. She'd approached him, well, maybe not exactly approached but she hadn't exactly refused, hadn't said no when he bought her drinks and walked her home — hadn't even refused the twenty he left on her desk when he split. Hell, he could tell she was the type who made it with every frat guy in Collegetown. She'd played the game well, listened to his divorce stories, office bullshit . . . gave him the soft soap about putting herself through school — well, she took him up to her room, right? What if she did pass out, so what, he would have made it with her anyway, what the hell? Easy. She didn't have to do a thing, probably wouldn't remember it in the morning. Yeah, he was the sucker, all right — she could buy some perfume or some books with the bucks. He didn't have to be a sucker, but he was. Easy touch. He liked the hot bite of the cigarette smoke in his lungs, he liked everything about the evening — even the fact that there were other people coming home late too, probably from nights close to being like his own. Yeah — good to be alive . . .

When he turned the silent corner off the Commons he noticed that the footsteps behind him were gone. Quiet. No apartments nearby and the bars were all closed, some stupid kid must be walking, stoned, not able to sleep, wired. Yeah, he'd been like that too, once . . .

If he'd been able to talk about it he would have told about the fog, how it became thick and choking. He would have mentioned how he felt as if he could grasp strands of fog, how he had tried to fight, fight hard but couldn't keep it away, off him, couldn't keep it from getting inside him, invading him, seeking every opening, insidious filaments crawling and invading and finally silencing his attempted screams . . . He never remembered the sting of the bite . . . only . . . the fog . . . if he could have told . . .

The monkeys were quiet. Slater pressed the lab door open carefully. Slowly. At once the primates were tight against the cold mesh of their cages, facing the intruder. No screams, only a high hissing sound, hysterical against the back of the throat, cut off beyond fear. The monkeys' canines were bared as Slater moved in more closely towards the rack of scalpels.

A dozen sets of brown eyes watched. She ignored the scrutiny, moving quickly, gathering rubber tubing, extra scalpels, a few glass vials. She tested the edge of one of the blades against her thumb, shuddering as the almost milky-pale liquid beaded up on the line. She moved toward the first cage, her eyes closed, her mind quiet. Carefully, coolly. The message she sent was simple, probing the animal darkness, trying to calm the whirling mass of terror.

The monkey threw itself madly against the back perch, mad to escape, mad at the unbelievable intrusion into its brain. Slater was sure, practiced. Again she probed the mind, inserting new images, planting soothing "memories," making it easy. Probing was the hardest with semi-tamed animals; what they held about the wild was clouded by captivity. As long as they didn't howl she could do this, could work them down, quiet. Only the howling of betrayal unnerved her, made her lose focus, clarity. With the wild ones the fear was easy to subdue. It was these who had grown accustomed to human handling that racked her with their Jesus eyes and their disbelief. Tonight her success was crucial. One mistake could mean the end of her appointment at the college. Christ, why hadn't they informed her of the number of animals in the lab? So much petty jealousy at these small schools — and this one — my Goddess a woman's college and every key position held by a man! She should be glad they even volunteered to give her an office. No choice, though. This was as close to the one she was seeking as she had been since the beginning. This time she would fulfill her vow. But she had to be sure, sure and very, very slow.

Slater opened the door of the cage and reached inside. Before the squirrel monkey could react she had it by two pressure points rendering it glassy-eyed, only semi-conscious. She would not let it slip into total blackness, precious oxygen would be lost. She needed the blood pumping, fast, awake with fear, filled with the liquor of adrenalin.

She tied off the small thigh, found the vein and lanced it into a clean vial. Three vials from different animals tonight, it would have to be enough. Carefully she eased the tourniquet off. Pressing a practiced finger against the incision she watched the flesh rejoin. Not even the few lost hairs would be noticed — simply a tiny scab, a scab the animal could have acquired merely by thrashing around in its cage.

Slater lowered the animal almost like a child. She could sense the unnameable horror in the small mind. She held the humanoid palm in her own, soothing it, calling it to sleep. She let the monkey's breathing regulate, and then, dropping the hand, withdrew. Twice more she repeated the process. Three vials full. She capped them and dropped them carefully into separate pockets of her smock. Revulsion filled her. Never never had she become used to the great blackness of these primitive minds. Fossey, Goodall, even Leakey be damned, she knew the truth of the half-lights, rutting memories, pre-verbal fear existing ever in the present. The animals closest to humans carried the memory of terror like the memory of God. She gently closed the last cage, shrugging off the necessary repulsion, bringing herself down to finally feeling only cold.

The other, untouched monkeys were silent. All furred backs were toward her, huddled. She cleaned off the scalpels and replaced them on the rack. She put the tubing in the marked drawer. No one would question her. This wasn't a government office, not even a decent research post. She was the new department head — their first woman — dedicated to research; published, schooled, credentialed. The very size and sophistication of the science departments at Weston made it the perfect occupational cover. Here she would be free . . . as long as she was careful.

The tall, handsome woman in the white lab coat switched off the lights as she left. She hoped this night she would have no dreams.

"Come on, Manilla, I've got to get to the library before it closes!" The senior stood in the hall, phone held at arm's length.

"I'm coming, Jesus, give me a break." Manilla slammed out of her room, mindful of the sound of shattering glass behind her. The Coke bottle on the window sill . . . terrific. Just what she needed, probably all over the report she was working on . . . the first for Slater. It would establish her as a serious student . . . it had to be the best. Slater. Something about her, a kind of depth Manilla found exciting but also distancing. She didn't want to look at it. Maybe it shouldn't be thought about openly, it would mean trouble. It wasn't the crush Ginny was so worried about, no, not even close. This was, well, unnerving. Manilla reached the phone, picking it up where her dorm-mate had abandoned it, on the doorknob of the laundry-room. Slater; she pushed the image, the name, all away.

"Hello?"

"Manilla? Someone dump on you, toots?" Ginny's voice was far away.

"Sorry. It's just that I'm trying to get this

damned paper finished and everyone here is an asshole. The library is closing early 'cause everyone's got the flu and I can't find another room to hole up in so I'm trying to write in this zoo — aside from that, it's terrific here." Manilla wanted to cry. The frustration over being separated from Ginny and having to be back solo at Weston, fighting, always fighting the lingering stares, the constant whispers, it was wearing on her. Simple exhaustion. Maybe everyone was just a bit more tired this fall. The fact that she and Ginny had been pulled into the proverbial limelight with their "cause celebre" the year before made it tense. There had been exhaustion then, but at first it was joyful exhaustion. The change had been slow, evil . . .

"Do you think it's, well, it's too debutante?" Ginny whirled around the room in the gown.

"Right, like my best dream." Manilla caught her, kissing her neck softly.

Ginny laughed. She pulled away, happy, so happy. It would work, it was almost over, the year finished, she could handle this final public event, even if her family was coming . . . she would be all right. Cornell was waiting — Manilla would commute back to Weston in the fall but she would like it in Ithaca, living in Ithaca! Both of them, together, truly . . . she would make it through this last graduation charade.

She had been forced into inviting them . . . into inviting him. Her mother had pushed her to it. Manilla didn't know, there was no need for her to know. Ginny would protect her from them as long as possible.

As far as they were concerned, she was simply another pedigreed female from the families of her clan, high-born, well-bred, perfect. She was a taller version of the virgin they'd sent to the nuns in Madrid fifteen years earlier. Precious possession, cared for, on permanent display. Her mother was comfortable with that. Her father demanded it. Oh yes. And she had fought his demands for years.

Olivia, Ginny's mother, had never understood the sudden frost which had grown up between her husband and daughter. Ernest rarely saw his child as she was away at school most of the time, yet he seemed to genuinely care for her. But in the last two years it was as if a great wave of cold had come over both of them, freezing her apart, away from them, and Olivia didn't like it. Ernest had grown distant from her, too.

She knew there was no mistress, a mistress did not fit the set he had so carefully constructed. A diplomat's wife, she would know in a moment if that kind of thing was going on. No, she was the perfect mate, the absolute hostess — a compatriot (with the help of good Scotch) in the best sense. She loved him. He should never have known that. It would have been better for both of them. Too late, too late. Her life was his. Now the frost, a killing thing on their numb bed. It was killing Virginia, too.

Perhaps if Virginia hadn't been such a fighter (another revelation — how little she knew of her daughter!), perhaps then the wintry edge wouldn't have been noticeable, they could have lived through it only slightly tinged — but Virginia did fight!

Outbursts, absolute fury whenever they had required her at social or family events during the last twenty-four months.

If her father was present there would be enough of a scene that it ended in a frozen truce — she would only come to them for Christmas. Even then she was ice.

Olivia did not push her daughter, nor her husband. Her husband was not a man to be pushed. He allowed no probing. There would be no discussion, no involvement. This was between him and Virginia and it would be dealt with some way. She was expected to wait, to watch, to keep warm as best she could. The bottled fire helped, and Virginia's schooling was almost finished. It was hardly necessary for a young woman in her position to go on to graduate school, but if she must play this dance thing out, Cornell was at least away from the City, safe. She would marry, of course. She would receive the first of her trust at thirty. There would be grandchildren. A cycle unwound and wound once more, slowly, carefully with grace and gentility. The spring would arrive, the snow would vanish. Olivia lived by these cycles, these rules, and they would do well for her only daughter.

Virginia needed taming. Weston, as a woman's college, had been exactly what they were looking for with its international, quiet reputation, its fine faculty, its size. There had been no fraternity entanglements, no "difficult arrangements" to be attended to; the women Virginia attended school with were daughters of other diplomats and political families. All in all, everything had worked and would work according to plan.

31

When October came and there was no invitation for Virginia's father to attend the traditional senior fathers' weekend, Olivia had not pressed the matter. Ernest had had two meetings in Johannesburg that weekend, and it passed without comment. However, when Virginia made no plans to meet them in Tokyo for Christmas, Olivia put her foot down. However, at the same time, the appointment for Ernest in Africa had come through and suddenly their lives were in turmoil. A recalcitrant Virginia would make matters bristly at best. Olivia had allowed her daughter to spend the two weeks "with a friend," not giving the matter much import for another two months.

Finally settled into the new embassy, the interviews and unpacking down to a manageable level, Olivia wrote to her daughter. She made it clear that if Virginia did not officially invite them to her graduation they would attend anyway. Virginia could cope however she chose. It was also of the utmost importance that Virginia reconcile with her father if only for that brief time. The major press would be all over them and Virginia should prepare for that scrutiny. If Virginia expected any financial help with her graduate work she would have to comply. Olivia knew there was no possibility of Virginia getting a grant or work-study, coming from the wealthy family she came from — and the rigors of a dance program precluded full-time work. This was her trump card. Virginia had to be tamed. This was the cost of being a woman, at least a woman with a future. If Virginia didn't learn it now she would be broken later.

Olivia had given up much of herself to become the perfect diplomat's wife. Her love for her daughter, yes, even that, came second. Virginia would not shame the family — not in front of national and international press.

A month later the official invitation, embossed in gold, arrived.

There was no signature, no personal card. It was, however, enough. For a week Olivia felt warm, free. And then, another envelope from Weston College. This time it was from the Dean of the College:

". . . and so there is a general belief here that your daughter may be involved in an unhealthy liaison with a younger student. Because of your family's special relationship with this institution, we felt it imperative to inform you at this time. No action has nor will be taken against either girl as we have no official policy regarding this situation. There is also little in the area of concrete evidence to support our beliefs, however . . ."

Olivia crumpled the heavy stationery and let it drop to the floor. Slowly, so slowly, almost prehistoric in her lumbering, she reached down and picked up the paper, carrying it with her to the liquor cabinet. Three Scotches later she knew she could never tell Ernest. She carefully burned the note in the agate ashtray on her desk. Then, sitting back, she closed her eyes against any more thoughts, closed her fist around the decanter of whiskey . . .

The reception line was slow. Photographers clogged the marble steps at the mansion entrance.

33

Students and parents were elbowed out of the way as press moved in for another chance at the diplomat. Africa was hot. He was hot.

Ernest saw the worried look of Weston's president and nodded to his security men. Six immaculate "tuxedos" ushered the photographers away from the arriving guests.

"Where's Ginny?" he growled under his breath, his arm tightening around his wife.

"She's late, obviously. You know how girls are . . . she's probably gossiping with her friends or touching up her hair . . ."

"I don't understand why she wouldn't allow us to meet her at her dormitory. My God, it looks, well, it looks damned odd. All of the other families are coming in together. For once I wish Ginny could conform!"

"Ernest, dear, please try to relax. She'll see you're upset and it will only make matters more difficult."

"She's the difficult one — we've given her a fairy tale life and all we receive in return is an ice-queen . . ."

"Look, isn't that Virginia now — getting out of the Fiat? Yes, oh, she looks lovely!"

Ginny's mother started down the stairs to meet her daughter. Ernest held his wife's wrist.

For a single moment she decided she would fight him — but it passed. She would wait for Virginia at his side — wait for her daughter to come to them.

"Thank Maggie for lending the car, okay?" Ginny pushed her shoulder against the Fiat's door.

34

"Wait a second, I'll get it." Manilla opened the driver's side. Ginny pulled her back.

"Don't. Please. You're not my servant." Ginny softly took her lover's hand.

"Nor your escort . . . Right, I get it, someone might see." Manilla sat back.

"I don't give a damn what they see. I just don't want you to have to go through — I don't know, it's just too complicated. It's seeing them up there, seeing him here, at Weston." Ginny's voice was breaking. "This is my place, my turf, these people, the school — he has nothing to do with it — nothing!"

"Gin, tonight won't change that. Jesus, I wish I could go in with you — face him, you know? Just give me the word and Secret Service or not, I'll rip the guy's lips off!"

"I believe you just might do that. Sorry sweets, seniors only, so just drive back safe. Thanks, Manilla. I love you." Ginny squeezed Manilla's hand for a second time.

"I know. I'll be waiting up."

"I'm counting on it," Ginny threw her weight against the aging car door. Suddenly there was a blinding flash. Manilla screamed. Ginny fell back inside, her shoulders banging against Manilla.

"Thanks girls, one for my family album!" The photographer ripped open the door again, took a second shot and was out across the darkened lawns even before their eyes cleared.

"Christ!" Manilla felt her heart begin to slow.

"May I escort you?" A tall, tuxedoed man gingerly helped Ginny from the car. She recognized him, or, at least, his style. Armed guards. Of course. Her

35

childhood memories flooded back — no toy soldiers, simply real ones, faceless, nameless, filling her house, her life.

He slammed the door and made a quick, wordless motion for Manilla to leave. She didn't think to question it. It was Ginny's circus now. Manilla peeled out, burning rubber in front of a dozen startled parents. The flashbulbs were still spinning in her eyes as she pulled a donut in the middle of the street. She'd leave, oh yeah, in her own sweet way! Fuck them! She put her foot to the gas and was gone.

"Where did that idiot buy her license?" Ernest leaned forward to peck his daughter's cheek.

Ginny reddened, trying vainly not to flinch at his touch.

Her mother caught the struggle, attempted a rescue. "Virginia, that dress is perfect! How wonderful you look, darling. We're so proud . . ."

"We better get inside, I think we're holding everyone up." Ginny moved into the foyer, not waiting to see if they would follow. Cameras clicked. The crowd parted. Her flesh crawled. "I can make it through this, I can, I can." Her thoughts were a mantra.

"You'll be seated at our table, of course." Weston's president took Ernest's hand. He was dwarfed by the seven-foot diplomat.

"Of course," Ernest answered, pulling Ginny and his wife aside.

College students served the seven-course dinner.

Every time someone Ginny knew walked in with a tray she cringed. She'd never been asked, in all of her years at Weston, to serve a seniors' dinner. How humiliating! It was straight out of a Bronte novel.

36

Ginny bit the inside of her cheek, kept her thoughts on Manilla . . . Manilla, her sanity, her anchor in this sea of charade.

Ginny watched her mother down another glass of wine. Olivia's cheeks were the same flushed shade as the liquid. Her gestures were becoming more animated, almost wild. In a few moments Ginny knew that her father would intervene — probably excuse them both for "some air." Everyone would smile, nod, be discreet. Ginny would be left alone at the table — the absence of both parents like a sudden vacuum. No one would look at her nor speak until they returned. She knew the script — had lived it too often to be unsure.

She checked her watch. Suddenly, Olivia was back. She was more subdued but the earlier grace was missing. A stiffness marked her steps. No one would notice, or, if they did, there would be no comment, not even an aside. This was the diplomat's wife. Ginny closed her eyes, her fingernails digging into the palms on her lap.

"Mother, why did you come here?" she hissed as her mother was carefully re-seated.

"My, this house is so nicely furnished. Have you ever been upstairs dear?" Olivia reached for her wine glass, smiling softly.

"Mother! You didn't have to come tonight. You know that! It would have been enough to attend graduation. If this dinner is . . . difficult for you . . . and him . . ."

"Why Virginia, what nonsense! What makes you say such a thing? We're having a marvelous time. It's such a treat to meet the faculty and administration after all of these years. And the President —"

37

"Is a crashing bore and a hypocrite!" The stress of the evening was taking an enormous toll.

"I don't want to ever hear you speak of your host in such a manner at his own table — now or in the future. You have been properly raised to know the distinction of propriety and poor taste."

"Mother, you know nothing about that man nor his sexist politics or . . ."

"And you know nothing of gentility!"

"Look at what you're doing here tonight, Mother! At least I'm honest . . . and sober." Ginny's voice was almost steady, almost calm. There, for years she had wanted to say it. Now, it was out.

Slowly Olivia turned toward her daughter. Her eyes were deadly. She gripped the edge of the table with both hands, her knuckles as pale as her face.

"At least I am normal." Olivia's voice was a harsh whisper.

"What?" Ginny choked back the burning in her throat.

"I said —" The strain of keeping Ernest happy, of holding back and holding back the disappointment she held for Virginia, the tyranny of the life she led, all of it was now unleashed by this night, this alcohol, this situation. To be confronted by her daughter, publicly, was the final blow. Her voice rose. "At least I am a woman — a normal woman."

"You have no right . . ." Ginny's voice was all but gone, as if a hand were wrapped around her throat. Shock, absolute shock, was riding her. There had been no indication that her parents knew. When had her mother ever cared about anything in Ginny's personal life?

"I have every right! When you left us you left us

38

whole, balanced healthy — and now — now I don't even know who or what you are! You're sick, Virginia, sick! How dare you criticize me, my life, your father's life, when you are so depraved?" Olivia was standing now. The table was in complete silence, all eyes cast down at their plates. Other guests at other tables seemed oblivious to the interruption.

Ginny felt herself shriveling. Every minute cell was screaming for retreat, for sanctuary — to get out, away.

Suddenly, two hands pushed Olivia gently into her seat.

"That's enough." Ernest stood above them, quietly.

"It is enough, isn't it?" Olivia began to sob.

"Excuse us, please, my wife hasn't been well. I believe our schedule has finally caught up with her." Ernest beamed at the President and the dinner guests. He gently helped Olivia rise.

"Stop it, stop it, you don't have to make any more excuses for me Ernest!" Olivia's mouth was sour with bile. The room swam in front of her, her life spinning out and around them like a mad stream overflowing with memories, feelings, sickness, slavery.

"I said it is enough." Ernest's face was tight.

Ginny didn't wait for the rest of the room to realize what was happening. She pushed away from the table and fled.

The hallway outside the dining room seemed altered. Her dress tripped her, trapping her, making escape too slow. Finally she brushed past the last bevy of students and reached the door. She could hear Ernest coming after her.

Outside the night wrapped a dark comforter around her. Moist, alive, the lake sang its spring

39

symphony, quick and warm below her. For the first time in her life she understood Manilla's need to be out — to find safety outside, in the woods, by the lake. Safety.

Ginny tore off her high heels and pounded across the spongy lawns. Safety.

Cars cruised Main Street, filled with college women or townies, all sneaking glances at the party on the hill. Safety.

She ran along the edge of the pines, cutting to the ravine, crossing the wooden footbridge that led back to campus. Safety.

Her feet were bruised, one toe bloodied where she had slammed into the walk. She hardly felt it, so intense was the horror propelling her back. Wilson's mask-like smile, his eyes wide with disbelief at Olivia's breakdown, her father's own well-clothed anger, a roomful of parents and classmates who would never forget, and finally, the absolute betrayal by a mother long since gone from her.

Safety. Manilla. Away from the monstrous party, the death watch of this night.

The drumbeat of fear grew stronger. Manilla would be in danger, too. Ginny knew the reach of her father, his absolute insistence that the family be decorous at all times, no matter the reality. He could destroy Manilla's life at Weston, disgrace her, remove her scholarship. He would make sure Manilla never finished a degree anywhere. They had to leave, get out of the country together, to Canada, or Mexico, maybe. Somewhere, somewhere safe. As long as they were together, away from the insanity of her family.

Ginny crawled up the moss-slick banking, skirting the shadows that led to the dorm. Flight had been the symbol of her life since she was ten — fleeing her family, her father. Ernest the diplomat, the seven-foot ex-collegiate athlete, the child-molesting monster with the enormous reach — all threats and promises and power — and her constant flight away. Even her coldness had not saved her — for in the end, his heat and his anger, his power could destroy anything. Now the monster was on her home ground, and he would come for her again, and also for the person she loved.

Ginny heaved the door open. There was only a little time now. She burst into Manilla's room. Her lover was on the floor reading, a half-empty Coke bottle beside her. The sane, comfy calmness of Manilla's room was too much. Ginny started to laugh, to become hysterical. She slumped down to the floor.

Ginny, the sweet dancer, in muddied dress and bloodied feet, hair awry, the golden mass flecked with twigs and pine needles, sweat pouring down her face, laughing on the floor . . . Manilla gingerly touched Ginny's cheek. "Gin? What?"

Slowly the air thinned, her breathing becoming regular, her heart easing to a more quiet rhythm. Ginny breathed. The hysteria burned away. A slow coldness was creeping back, a coldness that was always the herald of her father's presence.

Quietly, carefully, Ginny related the evening's events. She stopped only at the moment when she left the mansion and began her wild flight to Manilla.

Manilla handed her the Coke, not sure what to do. It could not sink in . . . Ginny's father . . . leaving Weston . . . danger . . . a letter about them . . . who the hell gave a care about them?

"Don't you see? My father is a very important

41

man in this country — internationally — and now more than ever the college knows how this could embarrass him. Wilson is slimy enough to want the satisfaction of knowing my father owes him a favor by keeping it quiet.

"I don't understand, Gin."

"She's known, forever, I'm sure of it. His coming to me — getting me alone — she had to have known. He wasn't careful, he didn't care, he knew he controlled her, controlled all of us. He never even asked me not to tell, the bastard, he knew I wouldn't. You're the only person I've ever told. Oh Manilla, it's all so damned ugly . . . I stopped him . . . I fought back, please, believe me, I hated it, hated him for it . . . hated her . . . hated her so much . . ." Ginny broke through the ice. Hot tears flooded her eyes, crept down her face.

Manilla held her, rocking. "I love you so much, Gin, so much," Manilla whispered into her lover's ear.

A knock on the door awoke them. The room was cold, the radiator off. It was light all around them. Manilla unwrapped herself from her quilt. The door slammed open. A man in a navy-blue suit and dark glasses stood there, his face lineless, distant.

"Who the hell . . ." Manilla pulled on her glasses.

"I'm sorry, Ms. MacPhearson, your father requests that you meet him at the Aura Inn. I'm to accompany you." The man stood just outside the doorway.

"She doesn't have to." Manilla stood in front of the guard.

"Yes I do, darling, it's all right. I know him. I know his men." Ginny's hands pressed wrinkles from her ruined dress. "I'll need to change. My room is in another dormitory. Meet me in front of the Main Building in twenty minutes."

Manilla was startled; she'd never heard her lover use such a tone of command.

"I'm sorry, Miss, your father says —"

"You have my word. I'll be there. I am not going to run from him again." Ginny swept the golden mass of hair into a neat bun.

"I'm going with her," Manilla stated.

"Twenty minutes, Ms. MacPhearson. The car will be waiting." The man pulled the door closed behind him.

"He means it. It's all we've got. You don't have to do this. You shouldn't come. He'll see it as a provocation." Ginny touched Manilla's shoulder.

"I've seen the movies, Gin, this is the U.S. of A. So his kid is queer. He can't kill your lover, you know." Manilla tried to smile.

"Yeah, well, like they say in the movies, they can make you wish you were dead. I'm terribly serious, Manilla, you don't have to do this with me, I can say you're gone, out of my life, I can lie to him, easily." Ginny stood at the door.

"No more lies, Ginny. Not from this point on. You aren't alone anymore. You don't ever have to lie again." Manilla kissed Ginny's hand.

"He'll call your family, probably already has." Ginny spoke softly.

"Yeah, I figured that, after last night. Well, we haven't been exactly close for a couple of years. They were going to find out someday anyway. Gin, maybe we really are each other's family now . . . right?"

"We've got fifteen minutes before the second wave

43

hits the door. Meet me at my room when you're ready." Ginny walked out, holding her head straight as whispers and stares followed her down the hall.

"So, you're the one. Interesting." Ernest MacPhearson coddled his snifter, his eyes flat, betraying nothing.

"The one what?" Manilla stood in front of Ginny, her fists hard against her thighs. Oh she would like to strike this man, make him scream.

"Very witty. I admire humor. Often it's the only way out of a sticky situation — and, my dear, you are in a very sticky situation. Sit down." Ernest sniffed the brandy.

The conference room was one of ten overlooking the lake. Manilla had been there once before, at a reception for a visiting painter.

"Virginia," Ernest said, "you're to come back with us today. We won't go through the sham of graduation, you'll come with us this afternoon. If you want to study the dance we'll arrange something abroad. But I warn you, you will come with me." Ernest put down the glass.

Ginny glared at the man. "I won't."

"I've called her parents, you know." He jerked his head toward Manilla. "They want nothing to do with her. She will leave Weston, her scholarship is revoked. There won't be another school in the country that will take her. I'll see to it." Ernest turned away from them, peering out toward the water.

"You can't do this, I won't let you do this."
Ginny rushed her father, grabbing his arm.

Ernest swung around, caught her shoulders and
held her at arm's length. His eyes burned into her as
he towered above her.

"Let her go." Manilla was quiet, her control
absolute, deadly.

"What?" He dropped his hands from Ginny in
amazement.

"Ginny told me about you — what you've done to
her. You filthy, perverted . . ."

"Johnson, leave." Ernest gestured the agent out
of the room.

As the door clicked shut his thin lips became
white slits against the scarlet of his chin and cheeks.
"No one will believe you. I'll have Virginia committed
— all it takes is my word. And you, I'll bury you.
There is no way that anyone will hear —"

"They've already heard. I have a friend on the
Ithaca Tribune who already has the story. Another
copy has been sent via college mail. If I don't show
up with Ginny at graduation the Dean of Students
will open the note and Ginny's diaries and read all
about you — dates, places, details only your daughter
could know, everything verifiable." Manilla looked at
Ginny.

"She's telling the truth." Ginny took Manilla's
hand, squeezing so tightly Manilla winced.

"Virginia . . . why? I love you, I've always loved
you. Why are you making up this . . . nonsense?"
Ernest's voice became wheedling and dangerous.

"Stop it! I can't stand it!" Ginny moved back, the
smell of her father's breath making her nauseous.

45

"All right. Stay here and rot. It doesn't matter to me anymore — you went away from me a long time ago." Ernest turned from her.

"It's not enough, Mr. MacPhearson. It would be too easy for you to come back after us. We want it in writing — a contract." Manilla kept her voice steady. "It isn't complicated — it simply states Ginny gets her trust fund and you continue to support her till it comes to term. No one touches my scholarship. You can't repair what you did to my family but you can stop here. You can stop despoiling the rest of your daughter's life." Manilla handed the envelope to the man.

"In return?" Ernest demanded, glancing at the piece of paper.

"You get no trouble from us," Ginny whispered.

"This is blackmail," Ernest roared.

"Don't talk to me about blackmail, father, not after all those years you held me prisoner!"

Ernest signed and stood up, towering over her. His eyes were lifeless, his face betraying none of his earlier fury. He held the paper at arm's length, making Manilla reach for it. Then he downed the last of the brandy.

Ginny never saw her mother leave. Her father did not speak another word to her. She kept most of the pain deep, away from her lover. Manilla could not understand, would never understand the complicated web she had broken. The ache in her was grounded in loss. Manilla had run from her family when she was only a teenager, escaping the doped burnout of a

New England factory town. Her lifestyle had been known and never spoken of. If her loss was ever real it was long since buried. But Ginny was alive in the slow-death pangs of her family. So she didn't speak of it often, and when she did, it was only with relief. Relief and a quiet desperation that made her hug her lover as if she were going to drown.

"Manilla, you still there?" Ginny listened intently to the quiet at the other end of the line.

"Yeah, yeah I'm here," she softly answered.

"Manilla, maybe you should just sleep, work later on when they've all gone to bed. You know you work better at night."

"What's the matter, Gin?" Manilla cupped the receiver closer.

"Nothing — it's just . . . dammit, I guess I know it's the paper for that new advisor. Maybe I'm a little jealous. I know how stupid that is but you've never talked about anyone the way you talk about her. Maybe I'm feeling left out. I hate it that you're so far away."

"I don't like it either, you know . . . Nothing is happening here, Gin. This prof is straight as an arrow — you know the type — the enemy. She doesn't even know me! I'm just glad the department has a woman to head it — that's all, finito. Remember Nestle from last year? I'd never finish my degree if I had him to deal with. Be glad, Ginny, for once I lucked out."

"You know, I remember when you'd cut all your classes just to hang out with me. What's happening,

47

Manilla? What's changing? I hate fighting you — I hate sounding like some floozy girlfriend — this is so damned banal! Forget I even called, just forget it!" The sudden cut off was too much. Already tired, strung-out about the coming year, the constant scrutiny of the campus, the ever-possible threat of Ginny's father, Manilla just slammed the phone against the wall. Grabbing her jacket she ran out of the stifling dorm and into the dark campus night.

"Fuck!" Ginny paced her loft, swiping at pillows, knocking magazines off the table. This was their first real fight in . . . how long? Longer than she could remember. For what? They knew going in that it was going to be a tough year. Hell, even their straight friends were fighting the rapids, trying to keep relationships above water. Why should she expect that their's would be any different? Manilla was just so sensitive these days, especially about school. She was punching buttons, okay, she could admit it, she hated it in herself. Manilla had never given her a reason to doubt. It was just that something about this new professor made her cringe. Something was happening, something hidden . . . even the air this autumn felt different.

Years back Manilla had had an affair with another professor. The professor left suddenly and Manilla had never forgiven the departure. Trust was not her strong point. Still, that had been a long time ago, two years before she met Ginny. Ginny had never been truly jealous — till now. Something was in the air.

* * * * *

Across the street, the top floor loft held a woman dressed in tight black leather. She moved the bamboo shade away from the high window, her ruby nails startling against the ebony varnish of the window frame. Like a heart's own blood, they throbbed there, drumming, drumming, keeping time to a pulse not her own.

The woman tossed back her mane angrily. It was still too early, so early, yet the hunger had come. Already the cold invaded her heels, made its slow progress up toward those strong sinewy thighs. Up, higher, into that cruelly cinched waist. Soon it would freeze the pit of her belly; so cold, so cold it would burn like an ulcer. If left unchecked it would work its way into her lungs, deep. The heart would fall next. The cold could paralyze that muscled machine even as it pumped alien blood through those frail arteries. A final chance, but if there was still no infusing warmth, no hot, long drink to revive and replenish the thousand-year-old cells, she would fall into an icy prison.

To those who might find her, her body's condition would seem deathlike. These humans had so few words! At that point even her mind would be deafened, unreading, unresponding and equally unfree. If it came to that she would be trapped until this planet spun out of its inevitable orbit and fell into its own star.

Unlike their fables, hysterical fairy tales at best, it was not the light of the sun, nor a wooden stake and crucifix that would end her, only the paralysis of starvation, the all-numbing cold.

It was solely through the killing that the cold might be halted. These humans had begun the myths — but before the myths she and her fold, in their god-pasts, had discussed what might be handed to the lesser race. The truth was too terrible; the truth of her breed held the icy lock of hell. The truth was trapped in a frozen tomb of rigid flesh, unable ever to regain the Center. The humans could not be told of this. Her breed, once so glorious, so vain, was now reduced to insidious seduction, to the human need for darkness and blood as fascination, attraction. That was how they lured them so that the cold might be kept back.

Her race could neither decompose and wed the earth nor ascend to the Center — it was the wager their first member had paid. Theirs was a limbo of ice and final destruction. Even the humans were better off. Oh she would have paid a far different price! She smiled at these musings, the irony — they moved over her like a first frost. They helped her wait. She must endure until the night was deep enough to be entered safely. Silently.

Her eyes fell on the golden windows across the street. She watched the dancer. Small one, delicate — something was upsetting her tonight, something about her lover, the dark, younger one. Yes their connection was strong. At first she thought she might take them both, but there was something about the younger one that made her pull back, hesitate. Danger? Perhaps. How? Rarely did a human give her more than a moment's concern — unless she had chosen to change the human, to re-make her. Of course they could never be equals — that was the fable her race created to help with the seduction, to complete it.

50

Such a tragic process when the lie became apparent! But, for a while, she could give them an existence that was comparable to royalty: full, euphoric, and terribly, terribly powerful. They had only to accept. And then, they had to be strong.

The only sadness came in the betrayal. When she was first born, those she chose attempted to hurt her at the moment of awareness. She grew to choose more carefully — though beauty was still a weakness. Men were the greatest threat, more dangerous and less predictable in their agnosticism. Like great brutes, their refusal to accept the obvious was loud, violent and less evolved than women.

In her middle time she had chosen both sexes. The power in the men's bodies, their animal vitality, pleased her, made her forget her own strength. There was a brief comfort in that. The women of those years were only delicate conquests, aristocrats mostly, and usually frail. She had had to reign her power in, becoming, in the act, tender. She had to dance the slow, burning waltz if they were to stay.

Men grew more dangerous when they guessed the truth. When they betrayed her they had already grown to be monsters, damned at the edge of the pit. She had been lucky much of her time. Today, to rely on luck would be folly. In these later years she had come to choose only women.

The humans had grown to surprise her — in the last quarter century women had changed, becoming obviously powerful in their own right. She began to seek out the strongest. Fine wine — she had developed a taste for fruit from these new vineyards and it was remarkably able to stand against the older, more refined years. The golden one across the street was such. An aristocrat, as in the old days, in both breeding and carriage, but more.

Her involvement with the dark, younger one added another dimension. Together they were quite remarkable. So much beauty, so much power! It moved her. The lesser race, these humans were the planet's ultimate burden. Still, every so often she had been made to pause, to take her breath in quick gasps. These two affected her in that quiet way. Before them (amazing so much in such quick succession!) there had been another of the Light. Aah, the last one, in the jungle, even now the remembering ripped her . . . It should not have happened as it did! So much needless waste! Why such a loss? Memory made her bitter for the first time in centuries, actually bitter. She had not taken a companion since . . .

Darsen's eyes did not overflow, not because there was no mourning, only because for her race there were no tears. A fist of nausea coming against the cold marked the memory. She pounded her talons against the polished wood. She watched through the window, seeing the effect of her actions, her feelings, upon the now-marked dancer.

Suddenly the young woman went down, holding her head in her palms. Darsen stopped the tapping, needing to be absolutely certain it was her power and her power alone which controlled the girl. The connection had to be secured. The moment the nails stopped, the dancer arose, shaking, as if coming back from a deep dream.

Darsen laughed softly, her momentary pain forgotten. It was time. Again. The fog had begun its litany. The dark would receive her. It was set in

52

motion, again, almost better than she could have prayed, almost beyond herself.

Darsen knew that on nights such as these there were still powers greater than her own. The thought both fueled and frightened her. She laughed again. It was the luscious terror of the hunt. Quietly she stepped into the waiting night.

Manilla didn't stop running until her heart felt as if it would heave itself from her chest. She was splitting in two.

Down into the damp moss, knowing she was close to the edge of the college gold-star golf course, away from the buildings, she fell. She pressed her forehead against the velvet green, pulling in the scent of mown lawn. What an irony. She had to be the only student who used the course after dark. It bordered her beloved woods, it marked the edge between college and what was left of the wildlands. Here, in the night, she was safe.

The forest saved her. As always. The haunted ground held her close. Strange to think of that now, even through the anger. Since she was a child she had run off to the woods. So often her uncles and father had found her asleep in the roots of some tree in the fields that bordered their New England town. Changeling, that's what the family called her, half-chiding, half-serious. She would lay away from them, awake at night, hear them whisper it: Something was just slightly odd about this child. Different.

Now they would know that those years of

wondering were justified. Ginny's father had seen to that. Of course this new knowledge had simply fallen into place for them all. There had been no phone calls, no letters, she hadn't even gone back there after that spring.

For years she had been the one to take care of the younger children while her mother was bedridden and her father on the road. It was she who had changed diapers, made dinners, sat telling stories until they all fell asleep. And when they were old enough to take care of themselves, when she could no longer stand the strangulation of that small factory town, she escaped. School, Weston, the promise of her art — freedom. They loved and resented her for it, they who had never left New England and its ghosts for one hundred years. When Ginny's father had made that fateful call it must have simply come together in a huge tomb of finality. She had never been truly one of them, their minds, beliefs, loves and honors. Always different, a forest child — even in the ruins of that rusted factory town — she had been wild, apart. Unnatural. Like any abomination, you cut it off, cut it away. She had been cut away a long time ago.

They never knew about the affair with her professor. Before Ginny it was supposed she was a virgin, getting a degree, coming back to town to marry and settle and possibly teach at the community college there. They had no idea of the intensity of her feeling for that older woman, how she had added to the great explosion of possibilities that Weston had begun inside her. When she left, she had not asked Manilla to follow, didn't even assume she would be interested. Manilla was a gifted student, a beautiful nineteen year old — another closed chapter. A deep-rooted cold had filled Manilla, a cold it took Ginny to unfreeze.

Ginny needed her in a way that didn't suffocate. Who but Ginny had ever given without demanding twice as much in return? Ginny burned for her and she had returned the hunger.

Her professor had taught her caution, had taught her sex — but it was Ginny who taught about love. They had been so bloody careful — or so they thought — until it fell apart. And afterward, only Ginny remained. Ginny was her family, her religion, her life. Ginny was where she wanted to live.

Manilla slammed her fist into the padded forest floor. Somewhere an owl called. A breeze touched the back of her neck, making her stop.

She slumped against a sugar maple, feeling the solid bark press against her, holding her up. Hallowed ground here. Indian ground ripped off and bloodied by the whites but never really theirs.

All of Weston, like Cornell, had been built on Indian land — stolen. She closed her eyes. The entire planet was stolen merchandise. Even the glare from the stars hurt.

This year was beginning to bite hard. How were they going to make it? What models did they have to tell them what was wrong, what would make their life right? How to keep it together, to finish school, begin careers, do their art? There were no lesson plans, no blueprints. What was so wrong, what made it so damned difficult even to talk on the phone? Ginny wasn't just angry about Professor Slater, it had to be deeper than that. What? What?

The stillness slowly began to filter in; the silence

was heavy. Even the breeze had quieted. Manilla opened her eyes, letting them adjust to the softened night.

Then, she saw it.

Carefully she moved into a crouched position, not sure, not ready to be sure . . . but it was there, the moon's half-cast lighting it from behind.

She tried to stop the scream that rose in her throat like sickness. She clutched the maple, needing its familiar ruggedness to steady herself. Like a child singing in the dark, she wanted the mundane, the usual.

The figure in the clearing did not turn, only kept to its task. Manilla was forced to watch.

The sounds of wet flesh seemed to overpower the night. The dying animal heaved a final sigh and was still. The figure continued — braced against the bovine, ribs filling both fists, the figure's face buried in the animal's neck. The blood flowed blackly in the deep shadow. There was no evidence of a weapon, no glint of metal, no powder burn. Yet the figure was too slight to have killed the animal somewhere other than the grass and dragged it here to feed. The next farm was at least on the other side of the eighteenth hole . . .

The calf was large enough to stagger a man. This was no man. The hair had fallen from inside the tucked bandana, hanging long and dark at the woman's back.

Manilla couldn't stand it. She eased herself to her feet, sure the woman wouldn't see her — she was feeding too intently.

Manilla began to back away, picking her way gingerly through the dead tangle of scrub and leaves.

Finally, the lights of the Student Union crashed brightly through the matte of trees. Always before the woods offered sanctuary. Tonight she prayed in relief at the feel of concrete under her sneakers. She tore down the road, back to Weston, back to her dorm.

Ginny answered the door sleepily. The red-rimmed eyes betrayed her crying. Her robe was half-opened, giving rise to the scent of powder and warm skin.

Manilla hugged her hard, not caring if the rough denim of her jacket scratched. For a long time they stood just inside the door, beyond tears, glad only for the comfort in each other's tangled arms.

"I tried to call you back," Ginny rasped.

"I was so mad, so hurt, I ran up to the woods . . ." Manilla felt the night come back like a fist to her throat. She needed to tell it, heave it out all at once, be done with it.

"I've begged you not to go out there alone at night — hunters, frat guys . . ." Ginny squeezed Manilla hard.

"Ginny," Manilla whispered back, "I saw something terrible . . . I don't know what . . . Maybe it was just a frat stunt . . . maybe a, a poacher . . ."

"Did you call someone, the Pinkerton men — the sheriff?" Ginny pulled Manilla into the loft, under the lights, examining her closely. Manilla wasn't someone who cried. It frightened Ginny to see her this way.

"An animal, someone killed an animal up there — a calf, I think, it was awful — still breathing — it was still breathing when . . ."

57

"Manilla, you know how poor some of the families are around the school —"

"No, it was a woman, a woman, Gin! And there wasn't a gun or a knife, just . . . blood, lots of blood and these sounds . . ." Manilla slumped on the sofa. Ginny sat close, holding Manilla's curly head in her lap.

"I was so afraid you wouldn't be here . . . The cops wouldn't believe me, they'd think I'd gotten some bad drugs or something . . . Ginny, don't leave me, don't even hang up on me anymore, okay? I get so scared these days, I get this terrible feeling that something is happening between us and I don't know what it is . . . I get scared that I love you too much." Manilla looked up. Ginny leaned down to kiss her.

Fingers grasped at clothes, pulling everything into a colored heap at their feet. The tangled scents of sweat, perfume, wet flannel and denim frosted the air. Their love-sounds filled the loft like jungle rain. Drenching, steaming out on the night air, into the fog-bound street, floating through to an open window. Their passion burning no one except themselves and one lone woman, clad in dark leather, slipping her key into a lock across the street.

Darsen entered her loft, smiling.

PART THREE

Upstate New York . . . still the present . . .

"You know the damned frat boys, they gotta hand out trouble first thing in the fall." The farmer finished his beer, pushing the empty toward Billy, the bar's owner.

"Out of hand is one thing, Mike, but killing a man's stock is another." The pinball serviceman put down his tools and looked up. He pushed the cap embroidered *Muldoon* back and stood. "Give me an o.j., will you Billy?"

Billy popped a plastic carton and poured. The juice was the brightest thing in the bar next to Billy's plaid shirt. Outside, metallic clouds seemed to be mulling a sneak attack on the lake.

Billy opened a bottle of Coke for himself, settling behind the taps. "They say there were witches around here, matter for reference, old man Weston's wife almost had a nervous breakdown when they were breaking ground for the school — told him no daughter of theirs was going to a school built on that ground — no way, matter of reference, right up there in the school library, seen it for myself, once."

Muldoon left the broken pinball machine and sat with the other two men, sipping the orange juice delicately. "You know, Billy, I heard stories too, come to think of it. Another point — seems like every few years since I was a kid in Weedsport some kind of ghost or weird thing is happened. Guess I never linked them up. Even the college stories — yeah, now that you mention it — remember back in early seventy-one, maybe seventy-three, a girl swore she saw Weston's wife floating around in a white dress up at the top of the campus athletic field. Maybe she was looking for the old man, huh?" Muldoon swiped at his bottom lip, missing a sticky drop at the corner of his moustache.

"Ha, that's a good one!" The farmer slapped the bar with a scrubby hand. "Billy, get me a brew, boy, ha, that's a good one!"

"Bad ground — that's what I say. Don't want to ever go digging too deep. Hey, they ploughed up all those skulls when they started on the school's tennis courts — I remember that one, way, way back in fifty-six — Indian skulls. Professors from Cornell and Hobart all coming up to Weston, all excited about it. Hell, if you ask me, it just proves what I always said, a bad ground. No sir, like I told my Daddy when I was a kid, there was no way I was going to be a farmer up around here, and I've lived it true." Muldoon finished the juice.

"Oh, don't give me none of that pansy stuff, Muldoon, you any better off fixin' them dumb-ass nickel eaters in all the bars around the lake? What you got to show your kids, huh? Bad ground my ass — ground's all we got around here. Ground was meant for farming. It's a damned good thing those Indians left when they did — this wasn't no place for them. Hell, half the game was shot and the fish fished out two hundred years back — wasn't nothing left for them here. They got paid for their land and the land pays us back now. It did my Daddy and it will my kids — what you gonna invest in for your kids' future? Fuse boxes? Dimestore bulbs? Ha!" The farmer wiped his hands on the backs of his overalls, hopped down from the barstool and headed for the john.

"Hello, boys," Billy said, "say what you want but I have to admit, this town is home for me. I like the girls, I like the village. I don't have to dig dirt or rattle bones to stay afloat — the Fango Bar is all mine, all paid for neat and clean!" Billy gestured around, taking in the pee-colored walls and broken pinball machine and marred tables. The black and white TV seemed to grin back at him.

"Well, if it was the frat boys Cornell should pay the man — two hundred was what he said it was worth this morning. That's no prank." Muldoon went back to the dead machine.

"Wellllll, who you gonna get to fork over the dough, huh?" the farmer asked, swinging out of the john. "That calf was a runt — wouldn't make it through the winter. Somebody knew that, picked it out sure as shit. Probably did Grayson a favor, now that I think on it. Killing it like that, he got the hide and the meat's still good, they tested it, right down at the campus — no poison, no worms — clean. Still it gives me the willies seeing something done in like that, like some lab experiment. Like when my kid cut up a big grasshopper for his science class. Damnedest thing — all the parts put out — and not much blood, not much blood at all. Like they bled a hog, almost — damn." The farmer sat back at the bar.

The front door opened. From outside the sun burned a cool hole through the clouds and blinded them. As their eyes cleared they saw the woman hesitate, then come in.

"Uh, can I help you, ma'am?" Something about the sudden intrusion threw Billy off balance. Like a blast of frigid air, the bar seemed to surround him with cold. What? What?

"If the ground is . . . bad . . . I'd say the people in this village have something to do with it getting that way. This was Indian land, still is Indian land. The Indian peach orchards were burned to the ground the minute the whites stepped ashore. They were never paid for what was stolen, they were never offered anything but murder as an option . . ." Still the woman's face was shadowed.

"What the hell you talking about, lady? We was just sitting here minding our own damned business when you come . . ."

Her head turned toward the farmer. Instantly he was silent. As if a strong hand had suddenly, from the inside, cupped his heart, stopping it for a split beat, then eased it back to its own rhythm. Shocked by something he had no words for, knowing only that this feeling was somehow associated with the woman in front of him, he dropped his gaze, grew silent, terrified.

"Look, I'm . . . sorry. It's just that I didn't mean to interrupt your conversation. I'm a professor at Weston — anthropology. We tend to get a little protective of the subjects, the people we teach — I'm sorry. I'm just looking for this morning's paper." Professor Slater stepped closer.

As her face entered the yellowed light of the Fango, Billy took his first deep breath since the door had opened. She was just a woman from Weston — a new prof — pretty young, good looking, just a college woman. Slater came up to the bar and stuck out her hand to Billy.

Muldoon stood by the pinball machine, watching. He had felt the cold, too. But something else, something, it made his flesh creep — made him mad. Like when Gwen gave him lip after a long day on the road, said something stupid, out of line, told him how to talk in his own house after working a sixteen hour day for her and the kids. Made him want to up and crack Gwen good, split a lip, see how'd she like to feel like she made him feel — like nothing. This woman — something about her made him . . . mad.

To the farmer's surprise, Billy shook the woman's hand.

"Professor Slater, yes, you must be one of the new ones if you don't know me. I'm Billy, the owner. Welcome to the Fango." Billy smiled uneasily.

"Glad to meet you, uh, Billy. I'm really terribly sorry to interrupt you, but the market seems to be out of this morning's Ithaca papers and someone seems to have pinched the one in the library. I was wondering if you sell —"

"Anthropology, huh? Well you must be the first woman in that department at the college. I know them all, you know, all the profs. Everybody comes here — we're all kind of alike, you know, family. How those boys treating you up there at the school? About time they get a woman for that department — should be a woman in every department. It is a women's school — right? I've been saying that for years . . ."

"Give the woman her paper, dammit!" Muldoon walked out from behind the big machine.

Slater didn't turn around.

"He don't have no papers here, miss." The farmer stared at a dustball on the floor, keeping his knees tight against the edge of the bar.

"Relax, Muldoon, the woman just wants —" Billy glanced at the big man sideways, something in him making him keep his eyes on the woman.

"I know what she wants, just give her the goddam paper you were reading when I walked in this morning!" Muldoon could feel his nails digging into his palms. He wanted to make two fists and smash the bitch's face, wanted to take her out. Something about her, the way she walked in on them, something wrong with her — like she was a rat and he was a hound in the barn. He wanted to tear her apart — wanted . . .

"Stop it!" Slater spun around, staring at the man.

Muldoon froze.

"The paper, yeah, I have the Auburn paper, that's all I got Professor, I'm sorry, what with all the commotion about the calf up at the school looks like Danny, the paper boy, didn't make his rounds . . ." Billy attempted to smile.

"Calf?" Slater didn't stop staring at Muldoon.

The man felt his stomach begin to grow acidic — something there burning him, beginning to move.

Billy pushed the opened paper at the woman. "About five this morning, Grayson up the road found his calf missing. He saw footprints near the barn and followed them over to the college. He found what was left of it."

Muldoon felt his belly crawling up his throat. She was burning his guts, he could see it in her eyes, something there, she hated him. She knew about Gwen, she knew what he could do, she'd read him the minute she walked in and she was burning him with it. He dashed for the john.

"Man can't hold his juice, what can I say?" Billy shrugged, the air around him cold again.

"What do they think happened to the animal?" Slater moved up to the bar.

The sounds of vomiting were only dimly muted.

"Well, a village this small, it won't happen again. The main thing is that Grayson got the meat for his family. Lots of small farmers around here depend on a calf to get them through the winter. It's just, well, kind of spooky. But they'll find who did it. Just you wait, Professor. And don't worry, Aura's a good town, bad stuff well, that happened a long time ago, right? Not too much anyone around here can do to change that. Sure I can't give you this paper? Or a Coke or something?" Billy reached for another bottle.

The toilet flushed again, followed by more retching.

"Why don't you give her some of that good juice you got." The farmer stuck his hands in his overalls, still staring at the dust on the floor.

"Why don't you shut up? Anything wrong with this juice Muldoon can take it up with the Lucky Market down the street — they sold it to me fresh this morning."

"I'll see if I can get a paper in Ithaca," Slater said. "I'll have to come by some night, Billy, maybe try your beer." She left.

Her perfume lingered, hovering over the odors of beer and cigarettes.

"Cold, fucking bitch." Muldoon staggered out of the men's room.

"What did she do to you, why are you so pissed, man?" Billy handed him a clean wet cloth from behind the bar.

"I know." The farmer didn't move.

"Know what?" Billy demanded.

"Enough," the farmer said, "enough."

"Something weird about her, Bill, something very strange." Muldoon slapped the cloth to his forehead. "Where does she get off telling us about this town? Or shaking her tail like that in front of us, looking like — like she looks."

"Like what?" Billy leaned over, noticing the cold was gone.

"Like that, man, just like that." Muldoon propped his elbows on the bar, cradling his head, his voice at the edge of tears.

"How did she know we was talking about the damned Indians?" The farmer turned toward the two men, his eyes wide, glazed.

* * * * *

Where? Where now? They'd found the carcass so soon — she was betting not until noon, maybe later. Crazed with hunger, the primate blood too little, she'd risked it. Never again. She couldn't wait so long between feedings . . . it made her desperate, unwary. Such a fool! For years she had been searching and now, so close, so final, and all perhaps lost because of one animal . . . Darsen, so close . . . her power influencing decisions she knew nothing about . . . these forces were deadly. Slater couldn't control the odds, couldn't hold everything together totally. She must slow down, be careful, realize she controlled nothing anymore . . .

The images of her bloodied hands, the hot, greasy scent of the entrails when she cut into the living animal, the last, pathetic gasp as it gave its life's blood to her . . . all rushed in on her now. The almost sexual release of the kill, hot, fast, so much power. Yes, there had to have been others there, decades before. Burning blood there, buried, the land so greedy for new blood, maybe centuries before; Indian land, yes, once, but even before the Indians, hundreds of centuries of bloody land, welcoming sacrifice.

That was part of the invulnerable power — Darsen's power — once her own. It rose over Slater and took her with it like a riptide, it pushed her under without air, the salt stinging of the blood like a scarlet ocean — that was how it had been the night before. So much, she knew so much now, so much she had only guessed at. Slowly. Darsen had grown more powerful and she weaker with their separation . . . but she was, perhaps, a bit more wise. Slowly. She would have to find another source of blood.

The town was bright under a graying sky. Ginny squeezed Manilla's hand as they found a seat in a quiet corner of the restaurant; it was rare having Manilla with her on a weekday. Under the cool autumn colors of the morning the night's argument seemed unreal. Waking with her lover beside her, Ginny felt as if it were a kind of omen, a good solid sign, a change that promised a new order. She was ravenous.

The food was hot, good. The two women — lost in each other, didn't even blink as the woman in a black poncho and dark jeans sat down across from them at the next table. She ordered coffee but didn't touch the cup once it arrived.

Ginny broke the reverie, glancing at her watch. "We better get to the Commons or you'll miss your bus — what are you going to do about your paper? Maybe I could call the prof and —"

"And say what?" Manilla smiled, gently nudging Ginny under the coffee shop table.

"Okay, so it's a bad idea. Seriously, I don't want you to get into trouble, you know? I worry, too." Ginny touched Manilla's hand softly. It was so good for them to have a stolen morning.

Outside the café, the street was crowded. Manilla scanned newspaper headlines. Local garbage: sex, death, politics, taxes — she flipped to the middle of the paper. On page eleven was a full account of the dead calf found at Weston College. Manilla dropped the paper. Where was Ginny? It was no nightmare, there had been something very wrong about last night — she had to find Ginny!

Turning around abruptly, she knocked into a wall of black wool. The woman faced her, long hair whipping across Manilla's cheek, stinging and drawing blood as if it were a fishline. Manilla gasped. She touched her skin, pulling her hand back stained with her own blood.

"My God, I'm so sorry, it must have been the edge of the poncho, let me help you." The woman moved in close to Manilla. Carefully, almost tenderly, the stranger wiped blood from the vicious scratch. "You surprised me when you turned like that." The woman's voice was unnerving in its familiarity — it touched something deep in Manilla. "Forgive me, please — morning isn't my best time." The woman's eyes were a cold, hard blue. They burned in their brilliance.

Manilla couldn't look away. The woman held a silk handkerchief to Manilla's cheek. Suddenly, before Manilla could protest, the woman was tight up against her, blocking her from the street. Manilla felt almost suffocated by the heavy black wool, now almost covering her face; by the heavier scent of some expensive perfume.

Lean, muscled thighs moved against hers. The hand held to her cheek was taken away; the woman's other hand had moved behind Manilla's head, cradling it, the fingers caught tight in Manilla's short curls.

Back, back, the strong fingers carefully pulled, unrelenting until Manilla's neck was fully exposed.

This was how Ginny kissed her. Suddenly, clearly, Manilla felt her lover's touch come into her mind. In a second her own mouth would respond, ready for the heat of tongue, full, hard, wet.

Manilla felt her breasts rise, nipples harden against the wool. The other woman pressed back, her softness moving, moving against the denim of Manilla's jacket and jeans.

The waves of heat eased, then rebuilt, moving her closer to the brick wall behind them. Manilla's palms were suddenly against the rough red facade of the building, pressed there for balance. Her brain rebelled at the intrusion, aghast at this forced dance, even as her body responded.

Behind them the street moved like a river. They were simply two dark stones at the water's edge. The current eddied and parted around them.

The woman held her knee between Manilla's legs, forcing them wider apart. Moving rhythmically now, the motion matching the growing heat, the pulse. The blood rose in Manilla, pounding at the temples; she was swollen, wet, open — against her will, but ready, ready for this stranger . . . a stranger, who, only moments before, had struck her, raising blood . . . And now . . . now . . . where was Ginny?

"Hey!"

For a moment the pale sun was suddenly blocked out.

Manilla's breath returned, hard and dry. The stranger who had been totally upon her was now clearly two feet away, next to Ginny. Ginny, the stranger; almost the same height, their bodies very similar, but similar in a way only a lover might tell.

"I'm terribly sorry, let me introduce myself. My name is Darsen. I seemed to have bumped into your friend and my poncho must have scratched her face — I was trying to apologize and clean her up, a bit — thank God it wasn't her eye." The older woman held out an exquisite hand to Ginny.

Ginny took it very, very gently. Cool, dry. Ginny didn't want to let it drop — so gently was the pressure returned. But she did, embarrassed at her response.

The woman's smile was like light. *My God, my mother used to smile like that, when I was little, before* . . . No . . . never . . . never her mother . . . Ginny snapped back from the memory.

"I'm, uh, Ginny, this is my friend, Manilla. Don't worry, she won't sue, she hates the law. Sorry we can't chat, we have to catch a bus. Thanks for helping her." It was like coming back from a dream. Ginny put her hand on her lover's shoulder, to ground herself. She touched the line of dry blood on Manilla's cheek and watched it flake away. There was no scratch. Ginny started to comment to the woman, but the woman was gone.

Ginny blinked, touched Manilla again on the cheek. "Are you okay?"

"Yeah, hear her? did you see her, too? Jesus, I mean . . ." But Manilla suddenly didn't want to explain anything.

"Maybe I shouldn't go back to Weston, maybe, maybe I should just stay here, have lunch with you later, watch you rehearse?" Manilla was dazed, sex-heavy, shaken; she didn't want to leave Ginny like that. Not after — what?

"Can't, sweetie, I have to work non-stop — it would really be a drag for you. Let's just get the bus, okay?"

"That woman, Gin, she was so weird." Manilla climbed into Ginny's Bug.

"You looked like a street kid, her dabbing at your face with a handkerchief. You had this really faraway look on your face. I was totally shocked when I came out and saw you with her. What lengths you will go to meet beautiful women — you brat!"

"Very cute, Gin." Manilla leaned back into her seat, feeling uncomfortable as if she had lied or done something to hurt Ginny. She hated the feeling. The morning was misting over, she was tired, she had to get the paper done, make up some excuse for the new prof. What she really needed was to get off the screwed up merry-go-round and move back to Ithaca and be with Ginny, just Ginny.

As they pulled into traffic, the sun went back into hiding. A copy of the *Ithaca Tribune* blew softly up the sidewalk, then came apart in sections, scattering, mixing with the leaves in the gutter. Slowly, it began to absorb the dirty water, the print blurring, the pictures pasted onto the curb, ragged, indistinct, one by one.

Manilla didn't stop once she was off the bus. She knew if she slowed down she would talk herself out of it.

The second floor of the Social Sciences Building was quiet. Lectures were mid-stream. Manilla approached her prof's office as if it were a morgue.

"Shit, she's already picked up the papers!"
A taped note on the door explained:

PROFESSOR SLATER WILL NOT BE IN
TODAY. HER MONDAY AFTERNOON
SEMINAR IS CANCELLED UNTIL NEXT
WEEK.

Good. She had a chance. Some slack at least. She could say she came by and the prof didn't show so she took her paper with her — an excuse, any excuse.

Tonight nothing would dissuade her from her appointed typing. Not even if the damned dead calf came walking up and tapped on her window.

She left the hall, uneasy but hopeful for the first time in weeks.

Ginny fiddled with the loft key. Her fingers were the only part of her body that didn't ache. Dance instructors were trying to kill her. Ha, they could all lie in the sun and die for all she cared. She slumped against the door frame and tried the finicky lock again.

"Locked out?" The voice was cool, smooth and very close.

Ginny spun around, unable to keep from smiling, caught like a kid trying to sneak back in after dark. Then she stopped. Her heart hammered against her; she pressed back against the bolted door.

"Didn't your mamma ever tell you it's dangerous for girls to live all alone? Didn't she ever tell you to have your keys ready when you came to your door at night?" The man moved closer, moving against her now. He reeked of old cigarette smoke and liquor, his breath nauseating as it hit her face.

All the self-defense classes she'd taken flew from her, each practiced, deadly move. Her knees, already weakened by days of long workouts that week, now barely held her up.

Your keys, use your keys. The mantra danced in her head. She couldn't move fast enough. He had her around the neck, squeezing there and lower, she could feel him growing hard, dangerous . . .

"Whaaaa . . ." He was off her, the sound of his head smashing against the brick wall was like a ripe pumpkin breaking. She was sick.

"Give me your keys." The order was curt, expecting obedience.

An immensely strong arm pushed her into the stairwell, slamming the doors behind them. There was no need. The man outside was not going to follow.

"Your phone! We need to call the police!" Darsen moved them across the room.

Ginny, still dazed, pointed. She allowed the woman to lead her to the couch. She didn't watch Darsen dial.

Finally Darsen hung up, came and sat beside Ginny.

"Sure you're not hurt?" Darsen pressed gentle fingers lightly at Ginny's temples. The morning's dangerous poncho had been replaced by a long black raincoat, the cut European, expensive.

Ginny noticed her head was beginning to clear. She steadied herself against Darsen. As Darsen held her the feeling was oddly familiar. Ginny didn't fight it. Only the sudden sounds of the sirens in the street broke the connection.

Together they went to the Police Station. They were questioned briefly while the intruder was sent to a security hospital, sporting a split skull.

"You two ladies don't weigh what he does, together. You know some of that Kung Fu stuff?" The desk Sergeant laughed at his own joke.

"Something like that." Darsen linked arms with Ginny.

The investigating detective walked out of the waiting room. "Well, we might be needing you later for more questions, maybe a court date, but you can go for now."

"Do you think she should go to the hospital?" The sergeant leaned over, asking Darsen.

"Paramedics assured us she was fine, no shock, and I know the man didn't get to her. If we could just get home now I think that would be best for both of us."

"You were lucky, young lady. It's rare to find neighbors who look out for each other. We've been after this guy for a long time." The detective's voice was heavy, parental.

Ginny shook her head in disgust at the tone. "Let's get out of here."

Back at the loft, Ginny handed Darsen a cup of tea. "Darsen, what can I say? I've already thanked you a million times tonight. If you hadn't been coming in . . . Brrr." Ginny sat on the overstuffed couch next to her guest.

"I hope this is the man they've been looking for, and not some other idiot. Well, at least we've officially met — a bit more formally than this morning yes? What do they call it, synchronicity? I call it charming luck regardless of the ghastly intrusion tonight. I like your friend, too — Manilla. She seemed . . . very strong. Something shining about her. Maybe this is karma, my way of paying your friend back for this morning's nasty bump?" Darsen reached out and touched Ginny's cheek. Ginny closed her eyes.

It wasn't lost on Darsen. "You have been together a long time?"

"What?" Ginny dropped her tea cup.

"Ginny, it's obvious, at least to anyone looking closely, anyone who knew what to look for." Darsen stroked the smooth cheek again.

"What do you want me to say? I shouldn't feel embarrassed but I do. We are very discreet, but we also want to be honest about our connection. It's just so damned hard." Ginny felt her cheeks flush.

"I understand — completely. I couldn't help but wonder if you might have room, in your 'connection,' for other people . . . room for sharing what you feel for each other." Darsen slowly let her hand drop from Ginny's face.

The effect was immediate. Like getting out of a warm bed in winter, stepping onto the freezing hardwood floor — something almost sad in the sharpness, the loss. Ginny tried to shake the feeling. My God — how close had she come to saying yes? How close to betraying Manilla with this strange woman . . .

"Did your friend say anything about us this morning, our little mishap? Anything at all?" Darsen's voice was musical, but there was an edge to it . . . almost mocking.

Ginny was very uneasy. She reached down to retrieve the fallen cup, moving farther away from Darsen.

"Ginny, I know how to read people — especially women. When you lead a life of constancy of motion, of shallow roots, you learn that to be able to read someone on a first glance is survival. Manilla is young and complex, she is also easily read. You like complexity, don't you, Ginny?" Darsen dangled the tips of her right hand into the honeyed tea and began to suck each one.

"Ahh, uh, you grew up traveling? Your family? Mine, too. My father is . . ." Ginny couldn't draw her eyes away from the long, elegant fingers, the ruby nails. She wanted to touch those delicate hands, take them up to her own mouth . . .

"I know who you are, Ginny. Today, well, there was something strikingly familiar about you. I was doing some research and I came across an article about your father in *Newsweek*. Your family, they're quite handsome." Darsen's hand was still raised, poised, playing out the game.

"Thanks, I mean, well, it's hard sometimes, you know? There are so few people who can understand. Growing up like that, it's different . . . When you try to answer simple questions about who you are, where you're from — or even just making decisions without having to weigh every single issue, sometimes it drives you crazy."

Darsen stroked her bottom lip, feeling Ginny watch, feeling the pulse between the woman's legs quicken, deepen. She had her. She could toy with her now — the line was cast, the bait taken. Virginia was a willing catch. Darsen could feel the heat beginning to rise, the scent coming off moist and hot from Ginny's skin.

"It's best not to let people in too close too quickly, I agree, I understand." Darsen reached out carefully. Her hand was light upon Ginny's thigh.

Ginny felt the touch, electric, desiring. Oh Christ, she was wet, hard with the quiet wanting, she hated herself for it, hated the power the older woman held. But she wanted to taste the power, too. So deep, her own hunger — where did it come from? Boarding school was a five-year-old, abandoned, misunderstood, a foreign country peopled with strangers? A teen-ager traveling with a ghost family, every school session in another country — locked out by caste, geography, language? Had the desire to connect with this tall, dark woman been born in the blackness of a night made deeper by her father's unwanted touch? So different from her hunger for Manilla — Manilla, the street-punked American cut-up kid turned artist who had somehow always belonged. This woman might envelop her, bring her to rest in a shared past, a shared history that she had never been able to fully explain. Darsen was an angel, an angel in the middle of the loft — an angel about to rescue the womanchild of her past. There didn't need to be explanations between them. This hunger was born of unadulterated recognition. Ginny felt the burn, the fury of the need.

"Would you like me to stay here tonight? Or, come to my studio — it might make you feel more, secure." Darsen stood, her body like one long black line.

Confusion poured in, the warm-bathed memory,

the instantaneous connection now gone scalding. "Darsen, I can't, I . . . if Manilla came tonight, I just can't, not now." Ginny closed her eyes, fighting tears.

"May I see you again, tomorrow?"

"Manilla will be working on a paper — a new advisor she's trying to impress — some bigshot anthropologist — maybe we could have dinner?" Ginny rose, standing close to her guest, feeling herself liquid. When had she been so wet so fast?

"Perfect. Red or white?" Darsen didn't touch the girl, moved calculatedly toward the door.

Ginny was hooked, unable to follow, but wanting to be pulled along. She wondered for a moment if Darsen had ever been a dancer. "Sorry, I, red, yes, red — I want to feel the wine. Something strong and red." Ginny's voice was a whisper.

"And complex." Darsen smiled. "I'll be here tomorrow evening."

"Good night."

Ginny watched from the top stair, watched the shadow that was Darsen move soundlessly out into the abandoned street. Ginny turned and rushed to her window, watching as the door across from her opened and swallowed the woman. Lights, muted, came on in the loft but Ginny could see little else through the wire-meshed industrial glass. Lights out.

Darsen, Darsen; when had there ever been such a name? Was this how Manilla felt about her new professor? Good God, no! The thought ripped Ginny. No — Manilla couldn't feel this way about anyone but her! Life was all too complicated again. Darsen had simplified feeling, simplified and rarified it. Without her everything seemed overwhelming —

81

enough — too much had happened — she couldn't think of what Darsen might mean, might come to. She was exhausted.

Pausing only to strip off her clothes, Ginny fell into bed. As she drifted it suddenly occurred to her she had never called Manilla about the attack. In the morning . . . simply too exhausted . . .

Darsen stood in front of the darkened glass. Her eyes glowed ruby in the shadows, piercing the night, giving her access to Ginny. She was indeed as lovely as Darsen had dreamed. Innocent, lonely for a past she could never recapture. Ah, too perfect. There was the bond with the other one, though — it ran deep. Still, it meant only that she must be careful. Delicious. Such pretty prey. If the younger one wasn't so unpredictable Darsen might risk both of them. There had been such a menage once before — but it had ended badly. No, better to play it out and settle for the golden dancer. All the more sweet, such a victory. Yes. Now with Ginny safely bedded, it was time for her to be back outside, time for the other hunt . . .

Manilla knocked carefully at the oak door. People could tell everything from your knock. Too hard and it communicated brashness, bossy unsophistication. Too light and it meant you were a timid finishing school refugee. Decided, well-spaced knocks got you into places. Yeah. She kept telling herself this as the perspiration ran down the front of her shirt.

"Come in."

Manilla opened the door. Her new sneakers squeaked on the polished floor. She cringed. How could Prof. Slater take her seriously if she squeaked?

"Manilla — it is Manilla?" Slater stood, pointing to a chair in front of the enormous rosewood desk. It was apparent that the senior was trying very hard. Slater fought back a smile. Something in the world still had to be right if she could be affected by innocence.

Manilla tried not to slouch in the overstuffed chair. She wondered if she should have worn her blazer, wondered if her shirt clashed against the flowered upholstery.

"So, your paper is complete?" Slater leaned across the desk, palm up, waiting. As her eyes met Manilla's there was a strange pull. My God — Slater moved back subtly. How long had it been since she had felt that spark? Ridiculous. Not now — not with a student . . . She sat down, avoiding the girl's eyes.

Handing the report over the desk, Manilla smiled. The smile was genuine, warm, reflecting in her eyes.

Again Slater felt the pull. Unable to stop it, her mind began a shallow probe — just enough to pierce the surface — her power so strong that that was all it took. Within that fraction of time she felt the lifebeat of the younger woman, felt it run along a path similar to her own, similar, perhaps years ago, but not now, not now. Too long she had probed too long, the student's sudden shudder made her reel back hard. If she didn't watch herself this college would become a coffin instead of a sanctuary. Too many mistakes. But this chance connection . . . it had been so long . . . Had she always been this lonely?

Manilla shook her head at the shock of the cold. "Sorry, Professor Slater, it's cool in here." Manilla noticed the delicate fingers and strong hands of the woman as she held the student file. Her heart pounded. So weird . . . She wondered if Ginny ever noticed people's hands.

Slater tucked the report into the file and put it into her top drawer. Better not talk to the student here — what if someone came in, suddenly? It would show on her face. What if the student suspected something? She had to read the files more carefully, be prepared. There was something here, she needed to know more before risking even casual contact.

"Manilla, uh, I have a proposition for you . . . I'd like to get to know all my seniors closely. This college offers that kind of intimacy between students and staff — I'd like to use the opportunity. Your interest in anthropology and art is of particular interest. I've gone over your transcripts." Too briefly, Slater thought. "And I'd like to talk to you at some length about your graduate plans."

Manilla colored deeply. Her entire time at Weston there had never been a professor to care about her — let alone what happened after she left.

Slater had a legitimate desire, more than the charge she was getting from the girl. It was important to instill a sense of camaraderie in the seniors under her care — it offered her additional cover, added safety. She couldn't deny that there was more she wanted to know about this Manilla — she needed to check back records, something in the file she had glanced at. It had snagged her when she was reading it but current events had pushed all else aside in her mind. Now she wanted to return and retrieve the records. There was such a touch of light around this young woman — a reason for caring again — or perhaps she reminded her of herself. A long time ago, yes, but there was recognition here almost tribal in its intensity. How to tell the girl that? As she made the offer she put out her hand to seal the bid. The meeting was over.

Manilla took the hand hesitantly. The palm was so hot she felt it move through her. She didn't want to let go. Christ, a lifeline made her want to hug the woman, this woman she hardly knew!

Slater used the moment to probe again — more carefully now — and this time she implanted a suggestion. She knew Manilla would come to her on her terms, there would be no risk to herself, there would be no misunderstanding between them. She knew the child could not resist, the power was too hideously perfect. It cut like a diamond, dazzling. Manilla was stunned.

"Tomorrow evening, my house, by the lake, for coffee, about nine p.m.?"

Manilla nodded, still transfixed.

Slater loosened her grip. Manilla's hand fell away. Slater felt the loss, turned away from the girl.

"Goodbye, Professor," Manilla said softly, moving toward the door.

"Yes."

The student moved sleepily out into the hall and away . . .

* * * * *

85

It was an old song. Ginny felt her hips begin that slow, pulsed cunt-thump-surrender, as Manilla had so rudely described it, moving with the current. Vulgar, yes, but apt. The blood flowed through the long legs, pulling down, lower, forcing her into slow heat, moving and making her move. She danced from that place — intensely. Like a lover's hands or lips, the music moved her on . . .

"Ginny, I hardly heard your knock, come in, please!" Darsen swung the industrial doors wide. Her eyes glittered in the fragmented light. Only her nails rivaled their brilliance — all else was swathed in smooth blackness. A silk envelope encased the lithe body. Ginny noticed, noticed everything.

The music seemed to go deeper; a finger at the throat, outrageous, suddenly frightening, a stranger's hand on one's breast; animal. Ginny leaned against the door to regain her balance.

"You look pale this evening. Just relax while you're here. You work so hard — will you allow yourself to be pampered for even one night? It's been so long since I've had a friend to prepare a meal for — let this be our night of friendship, Virginia?"

The name melted her down. She felt the tears on her lashes, tasted salt, was ashamed. How could she have distrusted this woman in the least? Darsen called to her as her mother had once called, when her mother was still . . . Ginny pushed the thought away with a swipe of her palm even as she pushed back a tendril of hair.

She followed Darsen inside, hoping the older woman had not noticed. The air was filled with the strange music that had first awakened her and then

lulled her — music and something else — incense?
Unrecognizable fragrance.

Ginny laughed, banishing the rawness that
threatened her. Manilla would be sneezing by now.
God, what was going on? Why was she here without
Manilla? One minute she was hot and liquid, then
wanting her Mother back, now wondering about
Manilla — she couldn't deal with any of it. She'd just
come in, have dinner, leave. No thoughts, no guilty
confusion. Darsen was her neighbor, had saved her
bloody life — they could have dinner without all of
this baggage surrounding them. Let the music and
the smoke fill her, let it drift her away. She sat on a
black leather couch and let its smooth skin soothe
her.

"The wine's been breathing a bit; may I get you a
glass?" Darsen held out a long arm, the wine in the
goblet the same jewel as her nails. Again, the effect
was not lost on Ginny.

Ginny took the glass, sipped delicately. She closed
her eyes and let the scent fill her nostrils, the
bouquet light and seductive.

"It's been a while since I've had good wine — not
that I think it's great to blow money on a bottle
when right in town some families are . . ."

Darsen smiled. She was so young, this dancer!
This was absolutely delicious!

Ginny flashed at how unsophisticated she must
sound. Images of her father blustering around the
house, then being so suave at a dignitary's dinner
table, swept over her. How angry he would be at her
crude comments — no finesse, the child lacked finesse
— how often had she heard that? What made being

87

with Darsen dredge up these ghosts? Ginny took a second sip trying to gently blot out the scene in her head. All day she'd held it together, routine discipline, she was a dancer, she knew how to push the body and then the mind when the body wanted to give, to banish any extraneous emotion until the dance was complete — but tonight she was beginning to unwind the feelings. It was normal, wasn't it — regression after attack?

"Virginia — you don't mind if I use your full name, do you? It fits you so well." Darsen moved in close.

"I guess not . . . No one uses that name except . . . I mean, not even Manilla — oh my God! With all my classes today I haven't even phoned her about last night! Excuse me, please. I've got to use your phone —"

"I'm sorry, Virginia, I don't have one here yet. Look, it's late. What good would calling her tonight accomplish? You will only ruin her sleep. The morning will be soon enough. Obviously if you believed you needed to call her and talk about the attack you would have done so by now. Come, sit beside me. Tell me what you think of my studio, my home."

Ginny was uncomfortable. She settled back uneasily. It was logical, it was true, it was more out of commitment than need that she felt she should call. She took the wine glass from Darsen hesitantly.

"What do you think of my work, Virginia?"

For the first time since arriving Ginny looked at more than Darsen. A quick intake of breath gave Darsen the cue she was seeking.

"So, you like them?" Darsen tilted her own goblet toward the enormous canvases surrounding them.

A jungle on all sides; steaming, full of dense shapes and colors, all carved from paint. The candles on the coffee table threw huge shadows over the space, fingers of light pulling apart the darkness.

"My work, this year's, anyway. I was in the Amazon Basin a few years ago but never could distance myself enough from the experience until recently. These come from my early sketches there. Have you ever been to the jungle, Virginia?" As Darsen leaned over to place her wine glass on the low table Ginny caught the flash of creamy breast; so much purity against the oily black of the blouse. Again Ginny felt the pulse between her legs; again her conscience split her from the feeling — she knew what Manilla would say.

No, this couldn't be the seduction Ginny played with — Darsen was too smart for that. She knew Ginny's feelings about Manilla, knew their promise to each other. Darsen was lonely, too beautiful for Ithaca. How could Ginny fantasize like that?

"I've, I've been to the Indian jungles and to Africa but never the Amazon." Ginny's throat was dry with desire. She fought it back. It was not right to be feeling like this about this woman . . .

"My art has taken me everywhere and I found the Amazon to be the only truly wild place left on the planet and I can promise you this is true. It is the core. The center. I want to capture that . . . in paint. It's incredibly elusive — like you, Virginia." Darsen moved in like a blur — her hand suddenly against the soft coolness of Ginny's arm. Through the skin, the eyes, Darsen could read the flood moving there.

"Darling, lovers should have no limits. I'm not here to steal you from your Manilla — only to offer you that which she cannot. Perhaps there is something I might offer her, also; sharing our lives makes us complete — extends boundaries that we once thought finite. Can't you see? You are both so lovely, fiercely proud, like two young Amazons. I'd like to capture you both, Virginia — not to separate you but to have you. For my art — for my life."

Ginny closed her eyes again. She didn't want to listen to the words, the words holding her in the arms of the music, moving her in time to the music and through the music, moving her ever closer to the woman in black.

Yes, she wanted to touch Darsen, to feel Darsen's touch. It was wrong. Manilla would be so hurt, of course, but the wrongness went even deeper. Ginny grew frightened. There was a coldness about Darsen — not in her voice, but in her eyes. Ice dwelled deep, it came off her in her unguarded moments — then it would disappear. Ginny shuddered, trying to throw the image off, away. Here there was heat, like a jungle, tropical passion. The paintings called it out — a mad brochure for an unexplored wilderness on the edge of a resort. It hinted at danger, promised adventure — but didn't tell you what was really lurking beyond the cabañas and gold courses. Darsen's loft was its center. Ginny knew the paintings screamed, lurched violently about the moment she took her mind off them, then rearranged themselves at Darsen's call. This was a haunted place having nothing to do with Ithaca or Collegetown nor anything in Ginny's past. And what of Manilla, what of that danger? If Manilla even suspected the

90

truth . . . They had always been honest with each other.

Ginny tried to focus but Darsen's voice bathed her, made her drift into the confusion more deeply.

"Manilla doesn't have to know right now . . . What is there really to know, Virginia? You are a dancer, a creature not bound by earthly rules, a thing of the air. And I am a painter. Manilla could understand that — Manilla is that, herself! All artists attempt to capture their Muse. Is it wrong, then, for this artist to try and capture you?"

Darsen moved closer to her. "Our life flows from our art — you, as a dancer, feel the truth of that. Each experience feeds that flow. How could I possibly hurt your lover if this truth holds fast? Let me touch my Muse, love my Muse, just for a moment? If I'm wrong, well, you are no child. You can stop me with a whisper — I will not be bitter. We'll always be friends, Virginia. It will not matter what we share or deny." Darsen bent closer. She knew her absolute power. Ginny's past, so easily probed, so easily read, had weakened the girl . . . it was almost too easy.

If Ginny had not been so beautiful the game would have ended. But the young woman linked Darsen to memories of sweetness and completion, a time when she almost hoped these humans had a chance . . . a simpler, more passionate time. It made Darsen's hunger rise, burning the room to a blue brilliance, making her touch like flame.

Carefully, slowly, Darsen leaned Ginny back onto the low, long lap of the couch. She felt the dancer's hard muscles relax beneath the soft clothes. Her mouth found Ginny's earlobe, began tracing the gentle curves, darting in, repeating the rhythm of

Ginny's breath. Darsen's sharp kisses pulled moans from the prone girl.

Ginny was not unconscious — her hands began to caress the back of Darsen's blouse, the black silk almost watery in her fingers. Finding two long slits, Ginny moved under the silk — flesh to flesh. Now, Darsen was driven.

Darsen moved between Ginny's legs, moved hard — made Ginny hot, so heavy, wet, open with the want. Ginny knew the woman would match her passion — knew the power in Darsen's body — so different from what Manilla made her feel — it had nothing to do with Manilla — nothing at all . . . Manilla . . .

Darsen's mouth was on Ginny's neck. It began the long sinuous glide from ear to collarbone. Darsen's lips trembled, she knew she was losing her restraint. Ginny's scent rose and filled her like a tropical rain . . . the scent of salt and jungle, hot, close . . . This one was close to her . . . Their hearts now began to share the same drumbeat . . . almost . . . too close . . . Darsen needed to slow it down . . . Speed was not part of this seduction . . . it should be spread out like honey in a trap. But the hunger was powerful and it drove her hard; her nipples were swollen, taut against the dancer's chest, her belly burning with desire. Tender, reddened, Darsen's deadly mouth began to transform — the lips pulling gently back, exposing, for the first time, their terrible secret. Darsen began to nip lightly at the petalled skin, to taste the essence that was Ginny . . . The climax this long, deadly kiss would bring was rising in her . . .

"*Manilla!*"

Ginny opened her eyes, coughing back a scream. Had she really shouted it or only dreamt it? She pushed roughly away from Darsen, clutching her dress against her flesh. She begged apologies, made excuses, it didn't matter now, she had to get out of there, that sham jungle, away from Darsen! Manilla — where was Manilla? She must find her, get out of the city and find Manilla tonight!

"*Virginia!*"

Darsen was trembling, almost weak from the intense break of current. She knew she couldn't keep Ginny by force. All right, let her fly, let her be damned! She stood to one side of the massive canvases, watching the dancer's retreat, her eyes glittering and as animal as anything in the dark room.

Ginny bolted out into the street. She slammed her loft door open and then locked it behind her. She shuddered, climbing up the stairs to the loft.

Her fingers shook as she dialed the dorm. Busy signal. Again she dialed, again, busy. Dammit!

Ginny ran to the bath, tore the faucets on, thanking God there was hot water. She stepped into the shower, soaping her skin until it ached, burning Darsen's touch off like sin.

Still, it was with her, an oil coating her, suffocating her. She rinsed the last of the soap from her hair and stepped out. Her dress was in a damp heap on the floor, the high heels under it. She knew she'd never wear them again. She kicked the pile violently, moving to her closet. She pulled on clean levis and a soft, worn sweater, searching for the running shoes Manilla had given her last Christmas.

Again she called the dorm. Again it came up busy. Ginny slammed the receiver against the table. Scouting amid the pile of papers and cups on the coffee table, she found her keys and ran downstairs.

She hesitated before pulling open the street door. If Darsen was standing there — no, she couldn't deal with the image. Please, God, not tonight. It was late and dark outside, but darker within. She knew that if Darsen moved from the shadowed street and asked her to come back, back to the wilderness of that studio, she would say yes.

Ginny heaved open the door. The sudden taste of blood from her bitten bottom lip shocked her. Only the clear night, black and cold but unbound by fog, greeted her.

The car was at the bottom of the hill. Ginny ran for it, dropping the keys once, like a bad movie take, expecting someone to reach down and pluck them from her.

The car started. No movie monster following, no sputtering engine. She pulled smoothly from the curb and headed out of town, toward the lake, to Weston and her lover.

"Be there," she prayed and slammed her foot to the floor, gunning it.

Light flooded the room. "Ginny!" Manilla exclaimed.

"Where have you been? I've been waiting for two

hours!" Ginny rushed across the tiny room and pulled the small woman to her like a shield.

"What are you doing here? What's wrong?" Manilla pushed away long enough to get a good look at her.

"I tried to call but you know this damned dorm . . . I took a chance and drove here — oh, just hold me, just for a minute, please!"

Manilla moved Ginny toward her bed, cradling her, not speaking. Finally, Ginny's heart slowed.

"Manilla, I had dinner with that woman — I felt I owed it to her because she saved me yesterday . . ."

"Steady, Gin, I don't understand what you're saying, I don't get it." Manilla, propped up on one elbow, stroked Ginny's hair, trying to read her. Often Ginny gave clues in her body which couldn't be said aloud.

"I wanted to call you right after it happened but she talked me out of it. She said there wasn't anything you could do right then so why get you upset . . . Last night, last night after class, it was late . . . A man . . . a man tried . . . I was so scared . . . just froze, Manilla, couldn't even scream . . ."

Manilla was horrified. "Did anything happen? I mean, are you —"

"If Darsen hadn't been there . . . that's why when she asked me to come for dinner I couldn't refuse. She's the older woman from the café at breakfast, remember?"

Manilla sat up, furiously protective. The memory filled her. The sexual bolt between her and that stranger, her face suddenly stinging with the remembered slash. She hadn't told Ginny everything

95

about the morning. It had been too clammy and unclear.

"She was at the café because she lives across the street in the new loft. Her name is Darsen. She saw the man, heard him grab me. She used some kind of self-defense technique — really creamed the bastard, then she took me to the police station, stayed with me. It happened so fast — then the dinner — I wanted to call you, I kept trying to call you!"

Ginny was huddled against the wall. Manilla leaned toward the foot of the bed, turning on the steam heat. The room was very cold. The familiar hiss of the radiator was comforting. No more explanations . . .

"Tonight I was just going for dinner, to talk. Her life was so much like mine used to be — the way we grew up — like the old days, or so I thought. She was kind, Manilla. She's a wonderful painter — these amazing jungle scenes — huge . . . Well, after a while I started to feel strange — almost like we *were* in the jungle and I was being, hunted, I guess. I mean, first the guy in the street then her. I felt so hurt — betrayed. She reminded me of, of, my mother . . ." Ginny's voice cracked.

The pain was choking, breaking her open. She sobbed against Manilla ". . . forgive me . . . I should have sensed it, seen it coming . . . I've never been unfaithful to you . . . Please say it's all right between us . . . that you don't hate me . . ."

Manilla fought her own tears. No anger. No rage — just the absolute white light of terror. Icy. Wasted. Its frigid hand pushed against her lungs. She wrapped her arms around Ginny, a human quilt, warding off this cold, flooding light.

"Ssshhhh, nothing to forgive, nothing happened, right? I'm just glad you're all right. I hate that I wasn't there — when that man — I would have castrated the son of a bitch! Thank God she was there — tonight was just a reaction, Gin, this whole year is like one giant chain reaction. It's not us, not really. Look, that woman, that Darsen, well, I didn't tell you the whole thing the other morning. It was so dreamy — I wasn't sure it had really happened. She pressed me against the building, tight, and before I could stop her you were there and she was like four feet away. There's something dangerous about her, Ginny — something psychotic. It's in her eyes. I thought I was tripping out when it happened. Don't talk to her, don't go near her anymore. Blame it on me — tell her you've got this very butch lover who'll take her apart if she tries anything. Then call the cops if she won't let up. I mean it. Or maybe we should just move out of the neighborhood. Maybe I could quit Weston, transfer, move in full-time —"

"Manilla, just stop it! You can't, I can't. Your scholarship — my father — I'll be okay. Any loft I can afford will only be in a worse section of Collegetown. I won't be pushed, Manilla! She didn't force me, it was unexpected, that's all. I miss you, yes, too much, more than I can admit most of the time. I shove my feelings down and don't deal with them until they implode. Will you promise to come down for the whole weekend, just spend it with me? Can I stay here tonight?"

"Of course, oh babe, it's going to be okay, it's got to be. We'll make it all right, I love you, Gin." Manilla reached out, wrapping her fingers in her lover's hair, pulling her into a kiss.

97

"There's never been anyone but you, Manilla, believe it." Ginny closed her eyes.

Manilla moaned as Ginny reached for her breasts. Slowly, maddeningly, Ginny's long fingers eased the fabric away from Manilla's body. Lips descending, coming hungrily to Manilla's tight nipples, Ginny felt the familiar heat rise from her own core. Gently, so gently at first and then knowing the effect on her lover, Ginny brought her teeth against the very tips just enough to scrape another moan of pleasure from the smaller woman. Delight, these breasts, so soft and full of this lean body, miracles, protecting Manilla's heart — so ridiculous maybe, but she could be silly and soft and melting here — it was their special passion now — she crushed her mouth against the luscious flesh, her lips flooded with rich spice and perfume, the musk of Manilla's response.

"Talk to me, Ginny, tell me a story." Manilla was almost crying with the ache of her lover's touch.

"There was a woman, an older woman, a beautiful woman who lived alone." Ginny felt the words coming through hot breath, the words allowing her to breathe, propelling them both on, tantalizing, prolonging this, their special game, "and she loved to collect beautiful furs. She knew it was cruel, maybe wrong, but she couldn't help herself." Ginny slid her sweater off, the sound muffled by Manilla's clothes already in a soft heap on the floor.

Her hands moved against her lover's darker flesh. Manilla echoed the movement in perfect counterpoint, only slowing if Ginny slowed, maddened and delighted now, crazed with the ebb and flow of it.

"The woman was beautiful, wealthy, and lonely because she didn't know she was beautiful." Ginny backed them toward the bed and then down, sinking and moving on top of Manilla, hard muscles against her lover's tender inner thigh, riding up and down there, open and flooded, pushing toward that hot, wet center, Manilla in echoed rhythm, moving and answering back, the chorus of soft and hard flesh in motion to the story . . .

"Faster, tell me faster, Ginny, please, please . . ." Ginny's hands moved faster, outlining the muscles on her lover's back, moving harder and faster and lower, down, down to that tight ass beneath her.

"Because the woman was alone and because she had those glorious pelts she would . . . she would . . ." Ginny gasped, sweat beading up, flowing onto Manilla, baptizing them in desire slick and fast and hot, she moved and spoke, a dance of heat barely able to tell it but telling it because Manilla asked and she would deny nothing, nothing to her.

"What, what would she . . ." Manilla was moaning, feeling Ginny's full body thrusts, the hands kneading, opening her, making her cry with the hunger.

"She would lie down on those furs in the dark or by candlelight . . . she would lie down," Ginny whispered hotly into Manilla's wet ear. Wet, wet, everything soaking and hot.

Manilla moved and bucked, wanting those hands and lips everywhere at once, wanting the agonizing story to fill her mind even as Ginny's hands and mouth filled her body, even as she wanted to fill Ginny.

"Slowly, in that warm darkness, the animal furs and scents surrounding her, slowly, carefully, she would begin to touch . . ."

99

"Where, where?" Manilla was trying to keep her voice from screaming, from having the dorm down on them in moments . . .

Ginny felt the hot wetness of them blend, stream, burn, she felt as if she was drowning there, a willing participant in this glorious destruction. "She would touch everywhere, make herself burn and tease . . . everywhere . . . her cunt, deep rubydeep, steaming, she would feel and touch and move deeply against those skins, the soft fur, alone, alone in the dark, burning . . ." Ginny's voice . . . almost gone . . .

"I can't stand it anymore, now, Ginny, please, now darling, so long, I've waited all night for you, please, please . . ." Manilla was biting into Ginny's neck, tenderly, holding back the wild scream building inside of her, almost feeling the animal fur and flesh, the jungle scent and savage softness of the stranger, Ginny, oh, her love, her life, oh above her against her, inside her, and she in perfect syncopation moving together through this voyeuristic dream of the lone stranger, the passion, theirs, the love, theirs, all the more because they were not alone, had only the pure flame of their hunger, the dream of the thrusting, the wave motion burning the bed, the room, each other till the fire burned even the fantasy and left only them, to the edge of the blue-white center, scalded and filled with it, sunk into each other, two as one, as one as one can never be, buried, silent past the screaming, breath stolen, brought back, together . . . that agonizing second poised on the edge of total meltdown, coming coming . . .

Outside, the moon waxed golden, its edges tinged ever so slightly with red.

* * * * *

Across the village, Slater shuddered. Darsen was close, closer than she'd been in five years of the search. She had to be within fifty miles. Tonight there had been some attempt at seduction. It left a lingering pain around Slater's heart. A drawn blade, almost used but not quite. Something had intervened, the act was left unconsummated. Slater needed to believe some power beyond her own was assisting in the hunt.

The moment Darsen completed the ritual, the second she drew another lover in, it would be finished. Their connection severed, Slater would die. She had to find Darsen before that occurred.

For all of Darsen's power she had not realized Slater was still alive. That accounted for the sloppy trail; Darsen did not know she was being hunted. Perhaps it was luck, perhaps the Goddess, something was aiding her — the only weapons she might rely upon.

Somewhere close, even at this moment, Darsen was moving. Slater would find her this time. She had to. The evil must not continue. Slater knew the truth: Darsen was the end of the original line. She had to be destroyed. So much evil would die once she was gone — so much evil had spread. The only exorcism that might save them all was Darsen's death.

Slater drank hungrily from the last of the vials. The blood was days old, unsatisfying, the rusty flavor more annoying than fulfilling. But she would make it suffice. She dared not risk another encounter in the lab. The howling of the monkeys would be noticed. No, she would simply push the insidious gnawing back even as it crawled from her center. Thank Goddess she was in farm country. Next to the jungles, this was the best location for her needs. With this young woman Manilla as an ally and alibi, this time the cards were in her favor. The student was smart, street-wise — and there was something more. Slater smiled at the recognition. Manilla was a renegade. She was hungry for a mentor — an older heart to give her more than what she had been dealt. Slater counted on this. She was drawn to this student, yes, the youth, the unabashed innocent belief in something beyond nightmare reality, maybe simple passion. It had been a long, long time.

The hunger was manifest in the cracking around her frozen heart — perhaps. Like a river in winter, the explosion of spewing ice, too much heat, a final, ironic thaw in her last season — all from this strange, darkling child. The qualities Slater once believed Darsen to possess, qualities she once held close in her own self, surfaced in Manilla. Her probing of the student, minute as it was, had proved this.

If all went as it must, Darsen would be finished — everything would come full circle. With that end, too, her own. This is how it had been eons ago. It was once more.

She looked out her window into the smoldering night face of Lake Cayuga, Cayuga burning up with moon. The ruby-lined satellite shifted over the waters of the lake, wandering. Slater closed her eyes, trying to remember what it felt like to pray.

* * * * *

The hospital was quiet. The ward nurse slept in front of the video screen. In her sleep she dreamed of a sudden snow, all-enveloping frigid. She didn't realize that the actual air around her had dropped almost twenty degrees . . .

There was no doubt she would find the room. He snored, his head wrapped in an enormous bandage. His breath stank of dry mouth and sleeping pills. She would have to be careful. She knew the drugs in him would make her drunk if she was not cautious — but her adrenalin was high. She would run the risk of the balance.

When he opened his eyes to the vision, lips curled, the canines clear and shining in that dead room, he saw it was the same woman. She had purposely not killed him outside Ginny's loft knowing she could come back for this. Such sweet victory — that he should see her wild and unveiled. The realization had been planted inside his brain.

Let this be the vision he took to Hell . . . And then, then there was a silence broken only by the sound of some large animal in deep and voluptuous suck . . .

Manilla found the note in her mailbox. Cream-colored stationery with a border of rust;

expensive, understated, unmistakable. She waited until she was out, under the pines, to open the note.

The faint scent of musk wafted from the envelope. She crumpled the sheet and tossed it into a trash can by the building. She took a few steps away, then stopped. She went back, pulled out the note, smoothed the paper gently. She stuck it in her jacket pocket, deciding to officially accept the invitation.

"I'm glad you've come. I hope you like fish — a friend stopped by with some snapper today. I thought it would be nice to share." Slater had met her at the door.

Perversely, Manilla realized she liked the feeling of almost being mouthed into the house, like a tender bite. The house itself was one of the oldest in the village — the architecture gothic as most of the lakefront property once had been.

"Are you chilly?" Slater helped the student take her blazer off, noticing the conspicuous lack of denim. Slater smiled.

"Not cold, just thinking how . . . ironic, I guess . . . it is to be here, I mean, for four years I've avoided dinner with professors. It always seemed so . . . trite. Or my own feelings of complication got in the way. Now, well, you're the most complicated professor I've ever had. Don't get me wrong, that's a compliment." Manilla blushed. There was a feeling of familiarity here — the sharp smell of tomato and garlic coming from the kitchen, the sound of the fire in the fireplace — even the imposing size of the room. Safety. Warmth. Someday she and Ginny might

104

have such a feeling: gratitude for the commonplace; home.

"Complicated? I've not heard that word used in conjunction with myself in years!" Slater led the student into the living room. Book-lined, floor to ceiling, three sides — it seemed an obvious place to start with a student. The huge fireplace dominated the fourth wall. Large enough to stand inside, it made the room glow.

Manilla took in the bookcases, feeling as if the room bulged with the volumes — as if it would explode into an avalanche of words, images. Yet she could breathe; no claustrophobia, only the overwhelming feeling of so many ideas.

Hardwood floors perfectly reflected the amber tones of fire; copper and brass lamps added more soft light. Everything was put together softly, gently. She'd forgotten there could be such quiet grace at the center of one's life — the familiar patina of a private space. These delights far outweighed the roller coaster existence she was living. Once the excitement was enough. Now she was tired. If only she could count on access to this room, and maybe this professor . . . Maybe this was what other students sought when they became friendly with faculty — a craving for quiet, light-filled spaces where there was much warmth, much ease. Maybe it was what the world craved.

Manilla felt the tears coursing down her cheeks. She wiped them away brusquely, ashamed at the emotion. Come on, it hadn't been so hard — not really. She and Ginny were revolutionaries, artists, a new breed! This was the very life they had passed on — it bred sloppy thinking, self-satisfaction, casual judgments. They wanted to be sharp; knife-like; close to the bone . . .

"Manilla, what's wrong?" Slater felt the wave of unhappiness well up in the younger woman. It had come over the entire room drowning even the Mozart on the stereo.

Slater crossed to Manilla — perhaps too fast — but she didn't stop with the possible risk. For whatever reason, this night she was open.

"I don't . . . I'm sorry . . . I never cry, I can't . . ." The feelings took over like a fist at throat or eye — so much hurt! Memories of younger times; the scene of dinner when her family was together; firewood in the middle of bad New England blizzards; a grandmother's touch while everyone else merely shook their heads at her 'wild ways.' Years since she'd let herself close to these thoughts . . . How much had losing her family really cost? Ginny was family now; and home. What if something happened to Ginny? The feeling of suddenly drifting away, being cut loose, abandoned, washed over her and Manilla could not stop the flow of tears.

Slater moved more slowly this time. She dropped strong hands on Manilla's shoulders. For a second the student flinched, then the tightness, the resistance melted.

Here was a depth Slater was unprepared for. Why in this one? Why now? Perhaps for the very reason that she was so close to the finale with Darsen. The dark-sided powers were intricate, devious. So much tenderness, a vast sense of recognition . . . promises of touch, passion . . . This younger one was on the edge of sharing the mystery Slater had carried for so long alone.

She could tell Manilla. She could explain the intensity, the horror of this split existence, and trust, trust the relief of the release of that secret . . .

She would not. Even as she held the dark jewel of Manilla she could not give in to the power — no matter the hunger or identification, no matter the longing and possibility of connection. Manilla must remain separate.

The years of solitude, the repulsive existence, the power chained, forever pushed back — all of it slammed against Slater. She could not cry — there was no confession that would unseal the tear ducts, no release for her. Manilla's release was pure vulnerability — like so much of her race. Darsen's dark release came from another place — it was the release of absolute lust and fulfillment. Slater was between them — without release.

She felt the ice around her heart break up — shift. In that shifting came the absolute surety that this was close to the end. Whatever she shared with Manilla would be part of the last act. The power that pushed her to take the child burned the night clear. She was close, very close — Darsen's angels wanted Slater away. They would not win. Gently she reached down and kissed Manilla's forehead.

"It will be all right, I promise, you're safe here. Maybe I understand more than you know. You must sense it — deep. That's what this is all about, Manilla. Trust me. Come to dinner now, we'll both feel better after we eat." Slater pulled a perfect Irish linen handkerchief from her pocket and dabbed at Manilla's cheeks.

Manilla allowed the unusual tenderness. There was no fight left. Meekly she followed Slater into the dining room.

After the second glass of wine, Manilla finally eased back into her chair. How long since she'd eaten a real meal? "Thank you for tonight . . . Ginny's loft isn't exactly a four-star kitchen —" She caught herself. What did Slater know about Ginny? Manilla had lived with the public knowledge for so long she had begun to assume that everyone at Weston knew. Maybe Slater didn't.

The sudden fluctuation in voice, the increased pulse; none of it was lost on Slater. She reached out a slender hand and touched Manilla's wrist lightly. The connection was instantaneous. The probe was in place. Manilla's eyes fluttered, she slumped further in the chair — focus was suddenly distant, fuzzy. Her mind opened its images to Slater. There was no question of holding back, none of explanation; Slater knew, could know, everything. Manilla was no longer in the room. Adrift — somewhere — the boundaries of the house had disappeared. Her body was intact but she was beyond it, Slater her guide. Whatever Slater wanted her to see, to feel, to listen to — Manilla was there. The immense freedom from responsibility was a massive drug, and Manilla didn't fight, not for a moment.

"Manilla, I know all about Ginny. Your files, your memories — all here for me to read. I won't play games with you — or at least I'll attempt to keep games from becoming a barrier — it's all right. I accept, approve. It must have taken a tremendous amount of courage for you both to stay, to fight, to go on with your lives. You've given up so much to remain together — your differentness cost dearly. I know." Slater felt the young pulse quicken — she was being drawn in deeper with each of Manilla's breaths. The probe was gentle but all-pervasive.

Manilla was lost in it. No more shame at the tears, no embarrassment over the disclosure about Ginny. Drifting . . . cloudy . . . Slater sat across the table from her and yet was right next to her . . . the touch at her wrist was exciting, warm. Slater was beautiful. Dark, strong, she must have once been an athlete; her body was lightly muscled and graceful. Dark hair brushed her collar. Her eyes were like the lake's own stones. Slater could be an older version of herself. The image cut her — sharp. They might be from the same flesh. Manilla was open, open very wide.

"Manilla." The thought was part of her, part of the student; to the young woman it would seem she was speaking directly, and yet her lips were motionless, silent. "Manilla, there are some things you must know if you will help me. I need you to be strong, to trust me. To help me in a way that will save all of us. There are many things I can feel inside of your heart, thoughts in your mind that are instantly readable. I trust what I see, what I feel. I could make you assist me. The power, my power, would allow me to wrest your will away and make you help, but I am taking the risk of asking. If you agree you will remember nothing of tonight, only feel a bond with me, a friendship perhaps deeper than any you have known — very different and oft times frightening in its intensity. But you will never be frightened of me, will never be confused by me nor, I swear, betrayed. You can accept or withdraw now — I offer you the choice. Your acceptance will mean that something absolutely evil in the world may come to an end — something that is so hideous there are no words for it. It is beyond human understanding of horror. You will be instrumental in stopping this monstrous force if you agree — but you will not realize the effects of your aid. Only in this moment in time will there be a revelation of the potential of your help."

Slater gripped the wrist of the young woman and the probe went like a needle to the heart of Manilla. "Watch. Listen."

A silent scream; pain, and then a panoply of the most gruesome images played out; from the Dark Ages through the Holocaust, African famines to South American death squads — every horror poured over Manilla. And what was most excruciating was the irrevocable certainty that she had been part of all of it; victim as well as victor; so many times she had said yes . . .

The images were torn back. A sense of drifting again — white and blue mist — warmth — the cessation of horror . . .

"In each there is a bud of this evil — a seed planted long before, needing only the right gardener to bring to fruit the evil. A monster to feed, to water, to nurture to maturity the destructive potential for cruelty that is sleeping in us all. We are not apart from the evil, Manilla, we are part of the evil — or more exactly, it is part of all of us. The depth of its sleep is determined by the choices, the circumstances we allow — but oh, the consequences of poor choice! Manilla, I have met the gardener who brings sustenance to these seeds — and know that every atrocity that has ever been committed on this planet can be traced to single decisions of individuals — decisions prompted and nourished by this virago . . ."

In the middle of the warmth of Slater's voice there was a burning cold — and there, in front of her, laughing, beautiful even as the dark is beautiful — was the face of Darsen.

Slater felt the recognition. The powers were equal; good and evil balanced for this moment; that which was attempting to lead her away had been momentarily arrested by a force leading her directly to her quarry.

Manilla had met the Dark One. This was no chance accident of connection. Manilla was sent.

Slater moved the image away, and the young woman moaned slightly, pushing against the power of the probe. Slater asked again for the help she now needed absolutely.

The answer was yes.

It was sealed. There would be time later to find when and where Manilla had met Darsen — that was almost extraneous now. More importantly she must fix into Manilla's subconscious the treachery of Darsen; the mundane history that made Darsen so dangerous . . . and the cost to anyone whom Darsen touched. She would share her own story with this young one and be finally purged of the secret. Yes, the final chapter was now in the writing . . .

* * * * *

"The Amazon — a living emerald broken only by a sapphire ribbon as we hurtled down toward the landing strip; and I was only a few years older than you, Manilla; a new PhD trying to make my mark and about to be changed forever; about to step into my own lush Hell." Slater suddenly shot Manilla into the plane — so real this power that Manilla could feel the worn seats flex as she leaned forward.

The probe would take them both back. Slater hadn't done this as completely ever before — but this night it was imperative. Simple words, images, none could convey the power that was Darsen . . .

"We packed light for the trip — my first into the bush, only for surveillance. If the tribe I was looking for could be approached, or was even known by the surrounding people, I planned to come back later, better equipped and better funded for a complete study. This time there was only the guide, myself and what could fit into the plane's cargo rack.

That first moment . . . Look, Manilla . . . out the window, see for yourself . . ."

Manilla smelled the airplane fuel, the old leather of the seats, the sweat of the guide, Slater's perfume. Gasping at the sudden altitude, Manilla leaned forward and touched the edge of the pilot's seat, feeling its solidity. No dream, no story, she was here, with Slater — above the jungle — and below was the Amazon River!

"Tighten your seatbelts, folks, landing's gonna be rugged," the pilot coughed back at them.

The guide put a hand around Slater's shoulder. She brushed it off, glaring at him. Manilla started to say something and noticed that he paid not a glance to her. It was real, for her, each smell, each snarling sound, everything — and yet they did not see her there; she couldn't communicate except to Slater. A strategic ghost — but one with feelings — Manilla felt very vulnerable.

Slater sensed the shifting fear rising inside the young woman. She pulled the probe back gently. Manilla experienced a warming sensation and then a blurring of everything in the cockpit. More dreamlike now . . . Yes, easier this way . . . She could handle it if it was a dream . . . Slater allowed the probe to settle Manilla's mind and then went back . . .

The landing was rough. The wings of the plane clipped the edges of the rain forest as it descended onto the pitted road. Perhaps not even a road, only a wash now used as a path through the bush. The plane coasted over the bumps knocking them about, spilling the contents of Slater's pack into the aisle. A camera, some film canisters, a few lenses, pencils and a bush knife bumped and banged around their ankles. Slater reached for the camera. The guide's huge paw grabbed her wrist and held it.

"Wait till we stop . . . want to break a finger or your wrist?" He attempted a smile. His teeth were long, white, dangerous.

Slater shook him off. She slammed back into her seat as the plane drop-dead stopped.

"We're here!" The pilot grinned.

"Where's the village?" Slater unlatched her seatbelt and sprang for the camera.

"No village around here, lady. Who told you there was a village?" The pilot pushed his cap over his bald spot.

"Johnston — you said . . ." Slater was trying not to sputter, trying to hold the rage in check.

Fear crawled over Manilla like a spider. The airplane prop was cooling and little pings and pops of contacting metal punctuated the jungle sounds.

"Look *professor*, you wrote and said you wanted a guide to show you possible sites of the Maneatos Indians. There ain't nothing close to anywhere you're going to find Maneatos — that is the point isn't it?" He stooped to avoid bashing his head against the cabin ceiling. He grabbed two khaki packs and moved toward the door.

"Closest town is Tefe, lady, and that's uh, maybe two hundred fifty, three hundred miles, right on the Amazon proper . . ." The pilot has softened his tone.

"The Amazon proper — aren't we supposed to be on the Amazon now?" Slater slammed her fist into a seat cushion.

"Well, you are, sort of. The river to your immediate right is the River Branco and it forks into the River Negro about seven miles down." The pilot checked the instruments. "God, Prof, they're all the same, you know? This is it — the real Amazon — just like the travel brochure says. Wild and wet — uncivilized, isn't that what you wanted? Lots of woolly bully geeks dancing in voodoo masks?" The guide banged the door open and jumped out.

The gush of air was almost iridescent with oxygen. Screaming macaws broke from the trees. The heat hit Manilla like a wet tongue.

"Johnston, I know where the River Branco is —

114

these are tributaries. I wanted the actual main river. If I'm going to test my theory I need —" Her voice was tinny, desperate.

"Oh, I know what *you* need, Prof — now let's just haul ass out of here — or don't. I get paid either way. No refunds — it's in the contract. I ain't going to lose my license just because some damned Yanque cuñuo goes soft." Johnston's eyes were brilliant blue-green, matching the jungle behind him. He looked absolutely huge in the full daylight. His hair spiked out, red-gold around his crown.

Manilla wanted to grab Slater by the belt, haul her back into the seat, tell the pilot to hit it, leaving the bastard Johnston behind to rot in the reddish mud. She tried to call out but nothing, nothing. All she could do in this place was observe, listen, follow. No voice. No touch. Simply a receiver.

"Ma'am, we all get a little bushy out here. Between the fucking revolutionaries, the Indians, scorpions and giant cats — it's bit of a hell, you know what I'm saying? You professors come out here, flash a lot of cash, make men greedy, come out with your film crews to do your National Geographics and such, well, you leave here and leave nothing — so, no disrespect intended, but fuck you, ma'am and your damned University! Just listen to the guide and I'll be back for you both in three days."

Slater tried not to shiver. The air felt very cold. These two were in it together. What had been promised, to the University, through the government — all ashes. These stupid, sad men — why had she thought it would be different here? She could go back, yes, raise Cain about the trip, admit she couldn't handle these people — get someone to come

115

back with her, arrange it all for her, or she could bite her lip and go on.

"Unload the rest of it, Johnston. You be back here when you say you will, same strip, or I swear the Embassy and whoever else bloody needs to know about it will have your ass! I mean it! People know where I am, when I'm due and who I'm with, so, have a nice day." Slater climbed out.

"Well ma'am, looks like Johnston's got your ass now so you have a nice day, too." The pilot spat out at them and waved as Johnston slammed the door shut.

The plane didn't wait for them to get off the path before it revved. Wings nearly hit them as it moved.

Just when Slater thought it would smash into a bank of trees it rose.

"That's it, we're home." Johnston shouldered his pack and grabbed a smaller bundle.

"Right." Slater slid into her own pack.

It was past noon when they broke through the last creepers and over-sized fronds. Before them was the mud-colored water of the River Negro. Slater pulled her boots off, leaving her socks neatly tucked into the tops — against scorpions and spiders. She'd read her bush books. Johnston grunted, dropping his pack to the earth.

Slater left him to slog down to the water. The air was buzzing with insects, some of them hundreds of feet overhead in the rain forest canopy. The birds were mostly silent in deference to the white invaders.

Slater's feet were scalded. She'd been toughening them for weeks, stalking through the salt marshes by the college, running five miles a day — but the dampness, the already mildewing material of her socks, the blistering heat, all had softened her feet to mush. Hot spots had rubbed into blisters and then popped — no blood yet but her toes looked as promising as raw hamburger. As she stepped close to the water she counted the number of large bubbles on the sluggish surface. She knew it wasn't piranha, too little action. Nothing moved as she threw in a stick. Carefully she chose her footing, knowing that a misstep could land her in the mud smack on top of an electric eel — six hundred and forty volts right up through the scum and into her foot. Fried. Upside down lightning storm, really. If she wanted to swim, best to hop over the shallows and float at the top. Alligators and kaman were either downstream scoping out otters for lunch or snoozing. If she didn't touch down in the water she would be safe from the giant catfish, too. Yes, risky business, but a kind of joy in it — she felt alive. If not for Johnston's onerous presence all would be perfect. She let the filter of light pass over her and felt as if she were already swimming.

"Best watch for cuts." Johnston stood behind her, picking his teeth with his fingernail. "First thing you know you'll get botflies taking a chunk out of you and leaving eggs — course then they eat their way out. You wake up and find some of your arm gone and your skin covered with the little darlings. Black flies are bad too, they cause river blindness — but then, you know that, don't you? Sand flies are the worst in my book, they bring on the leishmaniasis, you know, a dingy kind of leprosy, all your best parts drying up and falling off . . ."

"You just love it, don't you? Just get the hell away from me, Johnston, I'm no White Princess. Do your job and leave me alone." Slater turned away, the scene no longer inviting, only filled with the ominous buzzing and high whine of enemies.

"Well, since you're so prepared I'll just take a quick forty winks till the air cools. We'll travel till nightfall, pitch camp. Can't travel in the dark, now, can we? Even with a good moon, it's the fastest way to somebody's dinner, no matter what we think we know, eh?"

Manilla stood off, near a cassava plant. She watched Slater dry off her feet and move to her pack, a few yards away from the bivouacked Johnston.

Slater took out a first-aid kit and slathered dun colored cream over the tops of her toes, then neatly covered them with gauze and tape. The jungle sizzled around her.

She pulled netting out of the pack, tussled with the fine fabric, ensnaring as well as covering herself. The rest of the scene slowly bled away . . . the film fast-forwarded to night camp — Manilla finding herself seated on a log at the edge of a raging fire. The heat scorched her face. It seemed too much for the two explorers.

* * * * *

The night felt alive around them. Johnston was propped up against a tree with pistol, machete and bourbon around him, hoping to "stand guard."

"You're the one who told me there wasn't anyone or anything around for two hundred miles, right? You're going to burn us down with that forest fire you made." Slater moved her sleeping bag and netting farther back from the roar.

"Look, I've been hearing things all day, someone's following us. Didn't want to spook you, but it's most likely a damned Indian wanting some booze or my gun — so I'm just letting them know I know and we don't need any trouble, all right?"

"Jesus, I'm beginning to think I'd be safer with them. Don't lose it on me, okay Johnston? I don't know my way back there, not totally anyway, please try to keep it together." Slater's voice was a bit softer.

Braced by her tone, the man seemed to settle down. He would be all right. He could handle it, handle anything. Right.

Slater fell into an exhausted sleep. They had travelled non-stop for hours, the last of it through almost solid vegetation. The night was long, hot and alive with things moving just beyond Johnston and the fire. Manilla tried to watch with him but the dreamy mist held her and things moved slowly out of focus.

It was the silence which awoke Slater and snapped Manilla from the dreamspace.

"Johnston?" There was no answering swear, no snoring reply.

"Johnston?" Slater's whisper was a loud as a scream in the jungled bush.

A third attempt. Again, nothing.

Slater fumbled with the zipper of her netting, sure that whatever had taken her guide would pounce before she could release herself from the bag. Finally, she was free.

"JOHNSTOOOOOONNNNNNNNN!"

A monkey screeched back at her, rudely shaken from its own dark sleep by her call. She had crawled into her bag fully booted so now she didn't have to spend time fumbling in the dark for clothes. She stepped out and down. She felt a nauseating crunch and slide. Her flashlight revealed a spider the size of a baseball, mashed almost flat. Slater shuddered.

Moving toward the dead fire, she kicked at the ashes, trying to fan a bit of a flame. Carefully she nurtured a small tongue out of the face of the fire pit. She fed it carefully until a decent flame lit up the campsite.

Footprints, booted and not, surrounded them. No sign of struggle, no stolen pack, and not even an empty whiskey bottle. Slater knew Johnston wouldn't be foolish enough to ditch her in the middle of the night without his pack. And she hadn't slept so soundly as to be oblivious of a fight. But there was no evidence — not so much as a string — to show signs of struggle. She took a few steps into the bush. The howl of a nocturnal monkey sent her running back to the fire. She would sit tight. She would wait for daylight. She would wait for Johnston . . . The bastard . . .

The sun was broiling. Toucans yammered directly

above her, whether playfully or maliciously, she couldn't decide, tearing twigs and dropping them on her head. She must have slept. When? Her body felt as if it had stood guard, mindlessly, the entire night. A ringed kingfisher darted out of the jungle and headed for the water. Water — she was becoming dehydrated. The splitting headache was less from tension and more from lack of moisture. Picking up her water filter and her now-dented canteen she cautiously made her way to the edge of the River.

Macaws, parrots, giant herons, all blasted up and away from her as she grew nearer to the muddy edge. The brilliance of the green almost blinded her. So much saturated color — even the air was hued. She stretched out her arms, almost touching the rainbowed air. Johnston was missing, yes, and she was ill-equipped to be alone in this rain forest; still, the absolute energy of this paradise filled her. She was not afraid . . .

The water was drinkable, the filter was guaranteed — any parasites getting through would be commended. She wondered if First Alert Company would award a full refund posthumously. Slater struggled into her pack. Johnston wasn't coming back. It would do no good to just sit here. She wrote a hasty note and stuck it to his sleeping bag. She would travel southeast . . . eventually she would have to hit Manaos or at least some outlying villages. There was no possibility of finding the airstrip on her own. She'd report McGilly and Johnston to the authorities upon her return — demand that they refinance this botched expedition. She'd go with female guides next time and check their packs for drugs before they left.

Slater checked her compass, repacked it, and headed out.

It was late. The sun set like a deflating balloon in the forest. She had to make camp soon. She pulled out the compass. The cracked crystal showed spidery points in all directions. Dammit — it must have struck her knife handle or the camera when she hurriedly packed it earlier. Slater slung it into the woods. Something scurried away as she stepped out again. Hopefully it was an armadillo. She tried following the river for a while. Wasps and hornets molested her as she stepped into a muddy patch by the water. Swatting in desperation, she stopped long enough to realize that the forest seemed oddly familiar.

Slater walked along the fallen trunk of a giant tree — and came upon the deserted pack of Johnston. The footprints were still there and the dead fire untouched. A damned circled hike! She stripped off her pack and angrily collected wood. Well, at least if the guide stumbled back he'd know where to find her. By this time perhaps he would have sobered up.

The night was hotter than the evening before. Slater would not sleep. The moon rose, almost full, lighting the woods around her as brilliantly as the fire. It struck her that perhaps what was held back by the fire during the darker nights would not be so intimidated this night . . .

The moon went behind a cloud and with it the blinding light that obscured her vision. And then . . . the figure stood out darkly just beyond the fire's ring.

Slater gasped — tried to call out Johnston's name even as she realized it was not the missing guide. Reaching behind her for her knife, she tried not to breathe, not to betray her intent to whatever was watching her.

The moon slammed out from behind the cloud bank and the figure was gone . . .

All night Slater was on her feet, pacing, yelling, her knife in one hand, a burning stick in the other — taunting whomever to face her, angry at the insidious torture.

When the moon descended, sending the sun up after, she was still adrenalated. Stopping only for some beef jerky and a sip of water, she grabbed her pack, stuffing whatever food was salvageable from Johnston's pack. His compass, pistol, knife — all missing. Even his flares were gone. She was on her own. He was not going to find her.

The bush seemed to reach out and attempt to strangle her with each footstep. Four times she went down in the rotting vegetation, sending small armies of termites and ants scurrying out from beneath her. She felt nothing, not the stings nor bruises, not even the slashes from branches and undergrowth that had whipped across her face — nothing but blind panic as she crashed through the forest, trying to find safety in speed.

A few times she had felt "it" — knew something or someone was trailing her — pacing her — measuring her resilience. She would not give it the satisfaction, did not even stop for water when the canteen went dry, but pushed on, hotly, madly, fear overriding all.

She realized that often, in the past, what had seemed frightening was little more than problematic. She had never been truly hungry nor cold enough to fear death, had never been threatened with anything that would seriously thwart her life, had never been pursued in such a hideous manner — the enemy concealed — the danger a taste in her mouth but invisible, a poison gas about to choke her.

For hours she ran, trying to keep the river to her right — sure of only that — realizing that the river would wind back and forth and might actually have branched down. But it was her only direction. Finally the night caught her. There was sun and then there was no sun.

Day animals had retreated, the night stalkers were stretching. Somewhere, perhaps all around her, it was watching. It had kept pace with her and now was its hour. She stopped but there was no clearing to build a fire — her pack had torn open and all was lost except what was in her pockets: damp matches, a pen-knife, I.D. So, she would fight, then. Without fire, without real weapons, she would scratch and claw and not give in until it killed her. She would try to take it with her, if she could. The cold fury that came with the realization that this thing, this trailing monster, could beat her into exhaustion and now attack, unfairly, attack and take all that was her away, fueled her, gave her a second wind, new strength.

When the moon rose, fully round, awesome witness to her face-off, she screamed. It was not the scream of the victim. A final irony; she who had come there to find the Amazons had become one in her last stand. And then, Slater screamed again.

A tall, lean figure moved from behind the wall of green. Ruby eyes glittered madly, and then, a trick of light, went dark.

"I am here," a voice said.

At first Slater thought she was going mad. But the voice came again, quiet, intense, but not frightening.

"I am here. Come to me." *It* was the voice of a woman.

Slater dropped her knife. Tears crawled down her cheeks. English, civilized, a woman in the bush — not jaguar nor head-hunter — not even a jungle-crazed Johnston — simply, beautifully, another woman.

Slater stepped closer. The figure emerged to meet her, slender arms extended, ruby nails like so many tiny flames in the moonlight.

"Thank Goddess." Slater ran toward those arms and collapsed, heat exhaustion, dehydration and relieved shock coming to a head.

The tall stranger did not crumple under the expected weight, merely lowered Slater gently down. Carefully, almost tenderly, she raised a canteen to Slater's chapped lips. She bathed a dark cloth with more water and wiped the grime from Slater's cheeks. Then strangely, she touched the filthy thing to her lips.

Manilla felt immediate revulsion as she watched — felt, too, the movement of the woman as she turned and stared — not quite seeing but sensing Manilla's presence. In that second there was immediate recognition.

Darsen.

* * * * *

Darsen.

Slater pulled back from the probe, felt Manilla
recoil, then clench. Gently Slater softened the picture,
filming over it, misting it. She allowed Manilla's own
memory to take over. Reading the remembered
encounter in Collegetown between Darsen and
Manilla, Slater silently rejoiced that this risk with
Manilla was worthwhile. True, yes, yes. There was a
dark and deadly connection in what she had felt —
even in her attraction to Manilla. Some great power
was pulling them to a final confrontation, and even
in the midst of this probing, Manilla knew it too.

Slater moved her fingertips off Manilla's pulse. It
was crucial to time this perfectly; too easy to get
caught up in the telling too much. Manilla's mind
would implode at the reality. No, she would truncate
it, but still she must expose Darsen's insidious power.
Just a bit more . . . back, back . . . The probe gently
in place . . . Their pulsepound becoming one . . . Her
voice, her mind . . . her will . . . now taking over
Manilla's . . . misting in . . . drawing Manilla back,
back to the jungle . . . to Darsen's arms . . .
back . . .

There was a house; two stories, brilliantly lit from
inside; a porch swing moved gently in the humid

night air. Darsen held her close as they climbed the stairs.

The screen door swung open. A toucan on an ironwood perch hollered at the stranger. Darsen silenced it with a glare. The room seemed golden, unreal. Orchids and incense hung in the air, adding to her drugged exhaustion.

Darsen lowered her onto a soft couch. She brought a basin of cool water, some bandages vaguely smelling of peppermint.

Slater started to protest when Darsen began to loosen her blouse; the dark blue of the stranger's eyes stopped her. She could trust those eyes in this land of emerald and mardi gras palettes. The ice within that look cooled her fever, gave her delicate shivers. Quietly, she settled back, allowing the intense woman to undress her. Occasionally, a single nail would brush over nipple or navel, touch gently on inner thigh; yet there was no fear in her, no revulsion at this alien touch. Only ease, coolness, safety. She was like a baby once terrified, lost, but now found, returned home; home.

Months of struggle, of scraping money and letters together to fund her expedition; of dancing around old men and young men all peeking down her blouse or reaching up her skirt and secretly begrudging her every academic victory, the loneliness of her divorce — all melted now at the touch of this strange woman. Slater began to drift off, never questioning that this night, in absolute safety, she would sleep . . .

* * * * *

Days later, weeks? Slater seemed always tired, coming back from odd dreams, dreams where she ran light-footed through the jungle, laughing, always safe, with Darsen . . .

Darsen . . . whenever Slater would wake, the tall woman would be there, bringing her food, drink, re-bandaging her wounds, stroking her — a touch like that of the enormous blue butterflies she saw often in the air on the front porch — a touch she never believed she would find in this life. Darsen of the perfect teeth, the unmarked skin, the ebony hair. And then, when she woke, Darsen would take her for walks . . . so often at night, when the moon was new . . . the paths lit only by occasional light . . . Darsen began to teach her how to see with new eyes, and it was as if she had a different sense. She could see into the darkness . . . penetrate the bush with a glance. Had she ever been afraid of this paradise? When? Why?

Finally, she woke in a lazy afternoon, the sound of rain beating on the wooden roof, like the sound of tiny hands clapping.

Darsen was not with her. Slater got to her feet, smiling at the soft dress Darsen had put on her — the color of the orchids which surrounded the room.

"Darsen?" Slater called. There was no answer save for the rain.

Slater moved through the wooden kitchen then down a small hallway to the bedroom. The shutters had been pulled against the rain. A candle burned, attracting moths, lacing the humid air with the scent of beeswax. Briefly she watched the insects dive-bomb the flame. She blew it out. A single moth fluttered against her cheek, carrying the smell of burning upon its wings. Slater brushed it away.

"Darsen?"

At the end of the hall was a door she had not noticed before. The wood was dark, mahogany most likely, stronger-looking than anything else in the house. There was no lock. Hesitating only a moment, Slater knocked.

"Yes." Darsen was in front of her.

"I didn't see the door open, I mean," Slater stumbled in her surprise.

"I think it's the malaria — you've been through a lot these past few weeks. It will never totally be out of your system — you must always be careful, Katherine. Come in, please, I've been wanting to show you . . . my work . . . for some time. Come in." Darsen held out her hand.

Slater noticed a small silver ring on the left little finger. The silver was hammered, like moonlight, it shone softly on the elegant hand. In its center, like a perfect drop of blood, a ruby was cradled.

Slater took the hand into her own.

The room was half again the size of the original cabin. As Slater's eyes adjusted to the light she recoiled. Around the edges of the room were dozens of cages, and in each cage, bats.

"We've never really had a chance to talk about why I'm here or what you're doing out here — I think it's time." Darsen sat on a high-backed stool.

Slater sat next to her, in a lower chair. The bats were beginning to awaken, the day's early darkness triggering their response.

"You know," Darsen said, "the Finnish believe, at

129

least old land Finns, that our solid bodies let go of souls at night and those souls turn into bats flying around until morning when they return. Egyptians used different parts of bats for medicinal purposes. Their Indian counterparts still use bat skin for the occasional poultice. But the real draw for me are the South American and Central American stories — did you know that two thousand years ago in the Mayan culture their god Zotzilaha had a human body but the head and wings of a bat? He demanded human sacrifice — which was no mystery for the Mayans — he often appeared holding a human heart in one hand and a knife in the other. What is more amazing is that in Guatemala, in Zotzil, there is, to this day, a bat-worshipping tribe. The bat was long admired, the fear and bastardization only coming in later years through fiction and unnameable fear of the twentieth century — your culture, my culture. I'm studying these mammals. I'm an artist, a painter — working my way through the Amazon kingdom, as it were. I like to do field studies usually, but with the bats it's a bit difficult, as you can well imagine. I was attempting a night study when I came upon you, actually. It seems sometimes the bats do not want to soar with my soul." Darsen smiled, her ruby lips parting slightly, her hand touching the edges of Slater's hair.

Slater allowed the touch. The bats were only slightly unnerving. She trusted Darsen so completely that the explanation seemed more than plausible.

"Would you like to see my work?" Darsen was off the stool and across the room before Slater could answer. Perhaps Darsen was right about the malaria

— Slater's sense of sight and timing was more than a bit awry . . .

Darsen pulled back the cloth sheet covering a huge canvas panel. It was as if she had simply revealed a window to the jungle beyond the house. So perfectly detailed was the painting that Slater was momentarily puzzled that there was no sound . . .

"So, you like it?" Darsen was again beside her.

Slater shrugged, "Don't know what to tell you, I've never seen paintings like these before." Slater stared at the canvas jungle. Her heart was filling up with sudden pain, as if a fist were gently squeezing it, changing its rhythm. "Darsen, I have to lie down . . . I'm not feeling very well." The tears came in huge, wracking sobs. Not understanding what was making her feel or behave in this way, Slater ran from the studio, out into the hallway, feeling the walls of the house reeling . . .

When she awoke, Darsen was beside her. A fire was quietly sputtering in the fireplace. She was drenched in sweat.

"Katherine, don't try to sit up. It was another spell. I've radioed for help, it will be another week before bearers can reach us, maybe more. The only way in is up River and the rains have come early this year. I'm afraid it was too much, your stumbling on my studio, the animals — it must all seem so strange to you." Darsen knelt next to her, stroking her hair, running her slender fingers along Slater's cheek and neck. Occasionally the ruby ring would catch the firelight and gleam, like a silent animal, between them.

"Darsen, your work is so magnificent — I don't

know what to say. You've been wonderful to me — but I have to get back to *my* work. There must be people looking for me. And Johnston, my guide — never any sign of him . . . I'm confused . . . it all started poorly, this trip, so hard to get it started, I had to fight with so may of them to trust me . . . The dead-ends, so little belief in the Amazon reality, laughing, always laughing at me . . ."

"I know. When you were delirious, you spoke of the expedition. The radio confirmed who you are, don't worry. Please, my sweet woman, it seems we are closest to what is truth when it seems most difficult. Maybe, if you let me, maybe I can help. there are certain things I've stumbled upon while I've been out here, but later, later for all of this." Darsen moved closer.

Slater closed her eyes. She could feel Darsen's cool, clean breath. With each soft exhalation there was the scent of orchid. Darsen . . . She felt her heart beat strangely — and then the momentary fear was lessened. Darsen . . . The lips touched her own gently, moved toward her throat. Slater arched her neck. Yes — surprisingly, yes — she wanted this. So close now, so human . . . It had been such a long, long time . . . Yes . . .

Weeks passed. They were rained in, the river swollen with the season. Slater kept careful notes. Darsen had small artifacts to show her — had, indeed, made contact with the Manteos.

One night, as they lay together in front of the

fireplace, Slater stroked Darsen's ring. It seemed to wink at her, causing her to chuckle softly.

"There's a reason why you're drawn to it, you know." Darsen propped herself up on one elbow, stroking Slater's thigh with the other hand.

"Oh?" Slater purred.

"The myth of the Amazons turning men to stone — then dropping the stones into the River? A medicine man, a Hekura, gave me this stone when I first came out here. I took care of his daughter before she died of some kind of poisoning. He had never seen a white woman before — and never a woman as tall as I. He called me a name that translated to Amazon — or close to it. Before I left them he took me to his hut. He had a basket there with a clay bottom. He shook it. This stone fell out into his palm. He said it was great magic, it once had been the soul of a man. A woman warrior had turned it into a stone and threw it into the River. His grandfather had found it spear-fishing. the story had been in the tribe for generations, so grandfather recognized the stone immediately. The chief, I think, thought I was the woman warrior come back for my stone." Darsen kissed Slater long and full, her tongue caressing the inside of Slater's lower lip.

Still kissing her deeply, Darsen reached down for Slater's hand and slipped the ring onto her finger. It fit.

"Darsen," Slater whispered into the darker woman's ear, "oh darling, I can't accept it — truly." Slater pulled her hands through Darsen's ebony hair.

"You already have." Darsen silenced her weak protest with a slow penetrating kiss.

133

* * * * *

"Bad news, wake up, come with me." Darsen shook Slater to consciousness.

"What, what's wrong? My God, have you been out in the rain?"

"Just get your boots on and follow me, please." Darsen handed Slater a poncho.

It was pouring outside, the rain coming down from the tree-topped canopy as if the leaves were alien clouds.

Slater slipped through the rotting creepers and red mud, trying to keep up with the nimble Darsen. Finally, pulling up behind the taller woman, she stopped on the path.

"My Goddess — oh." Slater took one look and vomited to the side of the trail.

In front of them was an anaconda, its belly split wide and spilling out the partially digested form of a man — enough remaining to be identified as the missing Johnston.

"But it's been almost eight weeks — how —" Slater didn't look again, simply shook the words out.

"He must have been living in the bush — not a great feat for someone with a bit of experience. Maybe he made it to a village and came back looking for you after a little guilt soaked in. Whatever the reason, he got what he deserved. I saw the snake this morning, figured it was a small deer or a villager. After I got a good look — he falls out. Sorry, I'm really, for you, Katherine." Darsen put her arm around her.

"Don't leave him like that, please, Darsen." Slater turned briefly away.

"What else can I do? You've identified him — I'll radio it back. Do you want to paw through the slime for some I.D.? Anyway, the jungle will take care of it — it's too wet to burn. We'll come back in a week, set a marker. A man like that doesn't usually leave a lot of loving relatives. Don't worry, Katherine, trust me." Darsen started down the trail.

Slater never questioned Darsen. Here, with the rain insulating them, in the heart of the emerald bush, this was reality. Darsen was her angel. When Slater got back she could begin to decipher things. For now it was easier to live day to day. Her book outline was filling out enough to receive further funding. Darsen could illustrate it or it could become a collaborative effort. She was beginning to incorporate Darsen in everything, beginning to think of their life outside of the jungle . . .

"Do you love me?" Darsen was across the room, standing in front of the fire. Her outline seemed etched in gold. The rest of the cabin was blue-black. Outside, night owls screeched through hunting calls.

"Do you love me?" Darsen's voice was low, velvety as the dark.

"Yes." There could be no other answer.

"What about when we leave here — what then?"

"Darsen, I will always love you — there doesn't have to nay what-ifs. come back with me. I can't imagine being back there without you — you must know that."

"It isn't the jungle, then?" Still, Darsen did not approach her.

Slater opened her arms. Her heart was pounding. Images flooded her — lovers, her husband, all those who had ever attempted closeness — all melting and reforming, reforming back into the quiet, beautiful woman across the room. No doubt, none, yes, she wanted Darsen . . .

Darsen came across the wide-board floor.

In the dream-probe, even now in its lessened state, Manilla tried to pull away. She did not want to see this — too much, too close . . . Her heart began to match the heart of the women — but there was no looking away . . .

The candle was lit — it moved toward her. Slater closed her eyes. She had made a choice — the only choice. Her angel moved closer, carrying the candle.

The bed was soft, the fresh linen pulled tight. The white was almost . . . sacramental. Slater smiled, stretching out fully, the sheets luxurious against her hot skin. She could feel the flames. She was unafraid . . .

The candle was placed on the nightstand. Then swiftly, so swiftly that it took her breath away, she felt Darsen's light touch upon her brow. So light, light as the candle's glow, light as the night air wafting in closely. Jungle flowers, night-blooming luscious scents dripping fragrance on the air, caressed them both.

Darsen's hand traced a perfect line across her brow, the hard nails gentle. Slater wanted to laugh softly; she wanted to moan. The knowledge of the sacrament of these moments made her relax; there was no fear.

The dark woman was very close now, her long ebony hair trailing over her shoulders like black lace. Her eyes were as cold and blue as the precious stones they so resembled. Her lips were pale and fine; paler than at any time before that Slater could remember; pale and slightly drawn back.

Slater let Darsen hover over her, fingers like hummingbirds tracing nectar trails across her flesh. She felt her nipples hardening, growing stiff as Darsen traced the aureoles. Eager, so eager now, she could feel the dense and hollow pounding between her thighs; could feel the great vein carrying its fire inside the ruby-tide; the beat of her hunger, echoed.

Darsen . . . She called the woman to her. Burning with the want of her.

She arched her back, pressing her belly upwards. She felt the quick, hot tongue begin its descent. Her hands caressed and tangled themselves in Darsen's dark mane. No sound now, nothing but the pounding drum of heart and pulse. Sweat bathed her, made her mad with its salt tickle and burn; she could wait no longer.

She cupped Darsen's head and brought it down, down. Her moisture rose, her vulva heavy with the ache that would not be still; her heart seemed to have lowered itself and now throbbed there, the need making her open.

With a single movement that was all pain and pleasure, she felt those pale, soft-petalled lips part her own. They sank down, down into that most secret cave . . .

And then she knew the terror of Darsen's final secret . . .

Manilla pulled back hard, fighting for air, her own heart a drum. Slater kept her there, increasing the pressure at her wrist, changing the girl's pulse to her own. Almost finished. The final scene absolutely necessary . . .

In the morning Darsen remained with her — brought her her first drink. And she had refused the blood of the young tapir, retching at the truth.

For two weeks she had tried to starve herself even as Darsen explained the transformation, the story unraveling, crossing lines, giving new light to histories only hinted at in ancient texts. Finally, in desperation, Darsen brought a child, from some village down the River, already half-dead from Darsen's own deadly feasting. Slater could not finish the act. She slammed it out of the hated one's bloody hands and lay on the bed, sobbing, huge choking sounds all that was left of her human side.

Darsen screamed in rage, finished the child in front of her. And then left, moved away from her in a flash of light and horror, stripped of all human form — unmasked. Gone.

And once again, Slater was alone. Nights passed, days . . . until finally, the sound of flames woke her from her dreamless sleep.

The heat had caused the bedclothes to burst into flames. The entire house was on fire.

Screaming, she fled the room, only to find the shutters nailed from outside, the door bolted. Her strength gone from so long without nourishment, she could not break the door apart. There was no praying now, not after what she had become. Who would listen? And what would become of her after the burning? Darsen had never revealed it.

She knew pain. Her skin began to blister, redden. All about her hissed and sputtered. Spiders and scorpions scrambled from hidden cracks, dropped from the ceiling onto her. Batting them off, she rushed about. And then saw the fireplace. Laughing in hysteria, she kicked out the flaming logs and began her hellish ascent.

Smoke choked her lungs. Her skin was peeled back by the rough stone, her eyelashes and hair singed. She tasted the burning of her own flesh. Tighter and tighter the chimney grew — the top narrowing to keep out unwanted animals. She bent bones and sinew, realizing, in the middle of her own death, that she did not want to die. These weeks of horror, of absolute knowledge, the promise of power, of unending youth — realization of the monstrous choice she had made — in all of it she had prayed for death. Now, with the prayer about to be answered, there was some last act that must be attended to. A last evil to be put away. She must make it out of there to finish the greatest demon that had ever come to Earth. The death of Darsen gave her the strength of life.

Manilla watched in fascinated horror as Slater finally emerged. So much flesh had been burned or scraped off that her skin seemed to be black and red. Hairless, bent over like some hag, the woman fell from the flaming roof of the house, crashing through jungle to the sodden ground . . .

Slater let go of Manilla's wrist. Scanning, she felt the story inside the young woman's mind. Pushed back, beyond her dreams, it would remain there. Only the understanding that would allow trust would remain, a shadowed feeling to be called up when the time was right. Slater knew she could count on Manilla.

It had taken much out of her. Not in years had she been so drained. Slater rubbed her eyes, waiting for the young woman to come back, back into the home on the lakeshore, back to New York, Weston, the present.

The fire was low, coals sputtering half-heartedly. Manilla opened her eyes. The room was dark, cold. Manilla watched the professor switch on lights.

"God, how late is it? Have we been talking all

this time? It feels like I just got here, Professor. Must be the wine — I didn't pass out, did I? Jesus, I'm really sorry, you must think —"

"You didn't pass out, Manilla — you're just a bit drowsy. It's very late, we've had a nice evening, I think. We'll do it again if you would be so inclined." Slater smiled, walking to Manilla's chair, pulling it gently away from the table.

The student smiled back, sleepily. She stood, and then, totally on impulse, turned and embraced the older woman. Slater hugged her back, hard.

The night was blazing, cold. Geese honked warnings at the edge of the lake. They were keeping watch, keeping guard.

Manilla turned, hearing the sound on the wind, then wondering if maybe it was Slater she heard, but the door to the Professor's house was shut, lights out. She felt slightly stupid. She turned back to the road again, heading for her dorm. As she moved she no longer was tired, but felt almost easy, light. Somehow, in the muddle of everything she recognized that she wasn't alone, not alone anymore.

PART FOUR

Upstate New York . . . the present . . .

"Sheriff, I'm tellin' ya, no coyotes come this friggin' north this time of year — it wasn't no farm dogs neither! The chickens make a big fuss when any mutt comes sniffin' around. Last night nothin'! Fox, coon, those cluckers would've gone nuts and 'sides them animals don't kill like this. Maybe they'd take one, two hens but not a dozen, not pullin' the heads clean off. Look at them birds! You see any blood, Sheriff? I'm askin' you — smell any blood? No! Sometimes when I get to slaughterin' the smell gets so bad the wife makes me heave my clothes. No smell here — damn! Somethin' strange — just like that calf. I read the papers, Sheriff, I know what's been happenin'. You better do somethin' about it, you better damned straight find out quick and stop it!"

"All right Potter, I promise we'll do the best we can. Joe, make sure you pick up the dead birds — we better ship them over to the lab in Ithaca. Shit . . ." The Sheriff scratched his elbow.

The knock was light, almost no knock. She dreamt the knock and then was pulled from the dream, feeling the knock.

Ginny kicked the comforter off, pulled on her robe. She went blurrily towards the door.

"It's early, I know, but may I come in?" Darsen's voice was sultry from behind the door.

"Uh, you better not, I, I just can't, I'm sorry Darsen but I don't let people get away with what you tried the other night!"

The morning was pastel, heavy with sweetness. Ginny felt herself opening the door — watched in disbelief as her hand reached out and undid the dead bolt, the light flooding in around Darsen like a great golden halo.

Ginny was again drawn toward the dangerous woman.

"All right, okay, one cup of coffee, then you have to go. I mean it. I have classes today, all day. Dashing around is my usual routine so you'll have to excuse me if I'm not a perfect hostess. By the way, the other night, well, I told Manilla what happened . . ." Ginny held the statement out like a cross against a monster.

Darsen only nodded.

In the brilliant morning sun Darsen seemed lovely, safe. Ginny felt almost silly at her hesitation.

146

Darsen smiled. "I expected you would tell her, Virginia. You are lovers, after all, you should share everything. I bet she at least could appreciate my fine taste in women." Darsen's laugh was musical, close as touch, yet she did not touch Ginny.

"You think I'm silly and naive, don't you? Maybe I am . . . I trusted you, Darsen. I've been all over the world and I thought I could recognize a come-on in any language. But you — well, you're so damned smooth." Ginny moved to the stove to heat water.

She could feel Darsen's gaze burning into her back. She put the kitchen counter between them. Almost totally shielded by it, it lessened the connection.

"Oh Virginia! Please! I admit I was operating under a compulsion that was less than high-minded, but really, why do you think I came by this morning? I dropped in the other night but you were out . . . I wanted to apologize, explain . . ." Darsen left the comment hanging between them. Ginny dove for the bait.

"I couldn't stay here! I knew you were across the street, just waiting, probably watching for me. I went to see Manilla. I needed a friend . . . Darsen, how could you?"

Ginny's eyes locked with the older woman's. She realized her mistake even as she took a step closer.

Darsen was silent. Suddenly, in a breath, Darsen stood in front of Ginny, the long smooth hands touching each of Ginny's temples. Her breath was cool and sweet against Ginny's ear.

"Please, come with me, Virginia I want to share something secret with you, something wonderful . . ."

The phone screamed between them.

Ginny pulled back, feeling as if she were falling from a dream.

Shivering, she picked up the receiver.

Darsen moved in, then, deciding against it, retreated. It was not going to be easy. The energy — some kind of protection around this one. She'd been around for eons and had come to recognize the Power when it manifested. She had to concentrate to hide the snarl curling at the edges of her lips.

Ginny hung up and sat in front of her, ashen.

"It was the police . . . The man . . . the man at my door . . . they found him . . . dead . . . at the prison hospital . . . Something strange, the way . . . the way they found him . . . they're investigating . . . My God!"

"Not God, Virginia, something better. Ginny, really, are you sorry about this man? I'm not — the ugly bastard! What do they say about karma? What goes around comes around — or some such trivilization of philosophy — apropos here, no? Will you let me take you to dinner? What do you say? I still have some exquisite wine, we haven't finished our talk, please?" Darsen leaned forward, stroking Ginny's hair. The effect was hypnotic.

Ginny looked up, into the woman's eyes. They drove hard into her, pulling her up and close. Pressure, pressure on the aorta, altering her pulse, slowly, carefully, methodically, capturing Ginny surely.

"I, I . . ." Ginny fought the fear, felt her heart palpitate — she wanted to — to be with Darsen, yes. She knew she should run, get away, but also, she wanted to get closer. "Maybe, maybe this once, if we do something public, where there are other people around, maybe I could trust you enough for that — but nothing else, I mean it." The constriction in her chest lessened. Her robe slipped from one shoulder. Her breast was exposed. She watched, still hypnotized as Darsen's hand moved out and down. She watched as a bird watches a snake about to devour it. She could make no move to stop it. She wanted nothing to stop it.

Darsen could hear the pulse beating wildly at Ginny's throat and in the deep, fleshy parts of the breast. She knew Ginny's taste, knew the heady complexity of that wine. She controlled her passion. She let her hand move out and simply slipped the robe gently back into place.

"So, where would you recommend we dine?" Darsen's eyes were half-lidded.

Ginny answered dreamily, "A friend has an exhibition that just opened. Manilla can't attend, she has a paper due — can't make the final reception. If you like, we could go, at seven tonight," Ginny whispered.

"I'll be here — at seven." Darsen moved back toward the door letting herself out of the loft. "Virginia?"

"Yes?" Ginny called after.

"Don't be afraid. I'll be very good. I promise." Darsen laughed.

As the door shut behind her, Ginny slowly swam to the surface of the morning, coming back from a deep, quiet place.

Tonight.

* * * * *

"Well now, who's this?" David was anything but subtle.

"Introduce me to your friend, Virginia." Darsen let her gaze move over David. She would toy with this fly later.

"Darsen, David, David, Darsen. David is one of the finest art photographers around and one of my oldest and best friends. He's documented some of Manilla's work. Maybe someday — I mean, I don't like to put people on the spot but —" Ginny blushed.

"Oh, you have some art? Does Manilla know you're an artist? She's very good, you know." David cruised the tall, pale woman in front of him. He knew he had seen her before — but the memory faded as quickly as it had come. Strange, it wasn't like him to forget a face.

Darsen's mind released the probe. She didn't want David to remember the night she had first spotted Ginny at his opening.

"David! Don't be catty. Manilla knows all about Darsen — knows Darsen's my friend. She isn't cemented to my hip, you know! We do have separate lives." Ginny hated her defensiveness, knew David would see right through it. Then Darsen moved up close, her heavy perfume like an opiate. Edges were softening. David was mildly irritating, nothing to worry about. She was sorry they had come. She was probably safer alone with Darsen than out where rumors would scatter. True, she hadn't told Manilla about the reception — but the point was, did she have to tell Manilla everything? Besides, Manilla did have a paper due. If they couldn't trust each other around friends, they'd suffocate. She'd watched her mother go under like that years before. It was

150

absolutely proper to be with Darsen. And David, well, it was for his sake that she'd come in the first place — he could at least keep his mouth shut! What if he mentioned it to Manilla? Jesus — too much analysis. Better to be like Darsen — exist on impulse, deal only with feelings. Don't let anything get in the way. If Darsen really was like that. But she had to be . . . Ginny was sure.

She leaned on the arm of the woman in black calfskin. She was a pale edge against a darkening sky. She followed Darsen past David, leaving him gape-mouthed and hurt. For once, Ginny didn't care.

"I'm coming, I'm coming!" It was almost noon. Ginny stumbled through the midday heat in the loft.

She opened the door carefully. A delivery boy carrying an armload of orchids stood in the sunny street, smiling. She knew Manilla couldn't afford orchids . . .

"Here's the card, lady, sign for these, will you, I got the rest of them in the truck."

"The rest?" Ginny signed the receipt numbly.

As the boy unloaded the flowers the room came alive with the scent of jungle. Rain forest filled the loft, lush, heady. She was getting drunk with the scents as she opened the tiny gift card. In ruby ink a large "D" was scrawled — no message. She smiled. Ludicrous — totally inappropriate — but she loved it!

"Don't you think it's a bit overstated?"

Ginny whirled around.

"David! You rat — I'm surprised you dared come by after last night's little performance. No, I don't

151

think it's overstated. It's . . . well, it's wonderful. When was the last time someone filled your place with orchids?"

"Not as long ago as you might think, sweetie. Can I have a cup of java or do I have to come back with a bouquet?"

"Flowers or not, all you'll get is instant — help yourself, you old dog."

"Not old. But speaking of dogs — who was that greyhound you were walking last night? My God, Ginny, she was old enough —"

"To see through you! It's none of your business who I see. You know, you were never like this before Manilla." Ginny plucked a bud and ran it lightly over her lips.

"Before Manilla the only people I had to worry about were some cut-rate college boys. I wasn't worried. Since Manilla there hasn't been anyone else. You've made it very plain that you're taken. Rescinded that declaration lately?"

For the first time in two days a pang went through her at the thought of Manilla. "David, I'm only seeing friends, I'm not cheating, if that's what you want to know! I went with Darsen because, well, Manilla is busy with school and I didn't feel like giving up the reception. I'm tired of being alone, sometimes I get scared, David. I miss Manilla a lot and it gets to be too much. Darsen is the only sophisticated, intelligent person who doesn't remind me of school —"

"The only sexy —" David stirred the cup of coffee at the sink.

"David! Look, she's got some common experiences with me that Manilla doesn't share." Ginny hated the sound of her own voice.

"Pray tell." David sipped the coffee.

"Well, background, for instance. She knows what it's like being dragged around the world as a kid." Ginny pulled a stem of orchids apart, slowly.

"Honey, listen to yourself. You're the kid that hated your kidhood — remember? Manilla might not know first-hand what that was all about but she knows you! And do you understand her background any more deeply? Everyone's childhood stank, Ginny. What counts is who we are now — and from the way that woman held on to you last night I'd say she was interested in more than comparing baby books."

"Careful — you're stepping on things that can't be saved, David." Ginny was angry at him, even more angry at herself. No one understood. Childhood was not an illness one grew out of, like asthma; it was a constant, never-ending fever. It scarred one for life.

"Gin, I'm terribly sorry you feel like that. I thought we could discuss anything. I've watched dear friends make stupid mistakes, tragic errors — I've made a few poor choices myself in my day. You and Manilla are special — golden. You don't fit anyone's mold — so much intelligence, talent. For once I thought you'd met your match. Maybe it's an old man's need to see something remain sweet on this cancerous planet — I don't know. My first allegiance is to you. I loved your mother, once. I love you now. I can't stand by and watch you be hurt. I should know better — fuck this tiny tears routine — how about brunch? My treat. You're too late for classes now, anyway."

"You know me too well — oh David, I do love you . . . Just give me a minute, okay?"

David walked to the windows. He sensed cold coming in from the lake, the temperature would drop again by nightfall. An early frost this autumn.

As Ginny locked the loft behind them, she took David's arm.

Across the street, from her loft, Darsen was watching. She saw them move away. David. David. David. The pulse beat inside of her. Mantra demonic, she would use it, wait for the dark and use it against him . . .

"Sorry, she's out right now, can I take a message?"

The student was only half-listening, some strange dude from Ithaca on the line for Manilla — another weirdo, no doubt.

"Right, tell her David called; she's got your number? Got it man." The student scribbled the note and hung up. Dinner bells were ringing, she didn't want to be late. She stuck the note behind the message board on Manilla's floor — no time to hunt for a tack. No time to rewrite the thing.

As the dorm door crashed open, the wind ripped through. Shorn leaves blasted into the hallway, past closed doors, past the steamy laundry room, down,

down, strong enough to make it to the end of the first floor.

Two of the leaves swirled up and burnished the wall; brushing against the scrap of paper tucked against the message board. The leaves pulled it free, encouraging the note to join them in their tarantella through the dorm. Two ruby leaves, luring a paler sister away; farther, farther; gone.

"David? This is Darsen . . . Ginny's friend . . . I usually abhor machines but I'll make an exception seeing as the voice on the other end is so charming . . . I'm calling because I need a documenter and as you come with impeccable recommendations, I was wondering if your services are for hire. You know where my studio is . . . Would it be so crazy as to hope you might come by this evening? At least let me know so I can show you the work and give you some idea of its scope . . . around nine? If you can't make it, and I realize this is last minute, leave a message with Ginny, will you? We can arrange another time . . . If you can make it, just show . . . I'll be here . . . Oh, and David . . . money is no problem . . . I believe in paying people what they are worth . . ."

It was the only message all day. He'd let it play a dozen times. Each time the feeling increased — a kind of tugging, physical breath, heart, some sort of anxiety attack? He knew it was more than his imagination. And another thing, there was an obscene edge to it . . . almost pleasurable. He'd be playing with a viper, he was sure. Yet, if Manilla didn't

155

return his message, well, he had to take this thing into his own hands.

He loved Ginny. She was the daughter he would never have; the daughter he might have had, should have had. Once that had been a option — her mother had made him feel — what? A shiver passed through him as he realized the message on the machine gave him the same hot rush! Christ! Who was this Darsen lady? He had to meet her one on one — without the confusion of Ginny . . .

Outside, the street was foggy. The damp moved up from the lake like a huge reptile. David shrugged it off, purposefully glancing at Ginny's dark studio. Somehow, it made him relax. For a moment it crossed his mind that when Darsen's loft doors opened Ginny would be inside . . . He prayed, as much as he remembered how to pray, that it was only a weird image. Wild imagination.

The doors slid open, but no Ginny. A wire-caged elevator presented itself. Perfect. He smiled; of course this woman would have a cage for visitors. As it rose he realized, appearances aside, that everything was quite modern. Affected industrial chic — gauche. The door swung open and he was facing the tall, pale woman once again.

"I had a feeling you'd be free, David. I'm so glad. Do come inside. I think you're going to be pleasantly surprised," she purred, stepping into the shadows of the enormous warehouse.

Again, he couldn't refrain from smiling. She knew the right lines. Oh, he knew women like this . . . and not a few men. Digging in, preserving themselves at the expense of those around them . . . moving in when the pasture was green, moving on when it was dry . . . Yes, he understood her smooth moves. He also understood the underlying hostility.

Darsen sensed it. "I see you've brought your equipment — ready for work — excellent! I like men who don't waste time, especially where work is concerned. Would you care for some wine?"

He watched her melt into the darkness, her steps muffled by the scattered skins and hides covering much of the bare floor. Such a travesty! Like an enormous killing field! At least the air was cool — surprisingly fresh — almost hyper-oxygenated, like a greenhouse. He buttoned another button on his cardigan.

Darsen was behind him. "Sorry, I can't do anything about the temperature. As you can see, I have a number of valuable pelts. Also rare plants — they require strict environmental control. Show you around?"

David heard the click of a light switch. The loft was thrown into brilliance. He looked up. Above him, so entwined that they made a perfect canopy, were hundreds of tropical vines; creepers and flowering bushed plants, palms and fruit trees. Enormous pots lined the walls, huge trunks encased in antique urns. The woman had, for all intents and purposes, manufactured a portable jungle.

"So, uh, where are the animals? These the only survivors?" He didn't really like his own weak joke. The place gave him the creeps.

"Quaint, David. Actually, I don't like living animals. I can't bear the stuffed ones, either — so beady-eyed and watchful — but the furs are another matter. The plants add to the atmosphere, don't you agree? I've done a lot of furious trekking, one might say. This is the only environment I truly feel comfortable in — as I get older I get to indulge myself. I think you'll see how it feeds my art, David. Really, art is all — does that buy me a little forgiveness?''

He felt her watching him, his face, his throat, felt as if she had even exposed his heart; she was cruising him, my God, she would touch him . . .

Ginny was in real trouble. His instincts were right. She'd be sucked dry by this Medusa. He'd have a drink, take a few snaps — then, then he'd talk to Ginny with Manilla there. He'd lay it on the line. He took the glass Darsen offered — trying not to tremble.

The color of the wine was almost violet, the bouquet like rare wood. Ice-queen or not, she had money, class. He understood some of Ginny's initial attraction. But in the midst of it — such evil! How long had it been since he thought anything could actually be called that? He sipped the wine. At least the liquor didn't disappoint. Well, he'd have a second glass and take the bloody pictures.

She led him to the farthest edge of the potted forest. Pulling back some screens, she unveiled the most amazing canvases he had ever seen. Like the wine, the work was complex, rare, almost transparent. Burning, like underwater animals that grow luminous in the dark, the colors leapt at him, came alive. David was transfixed. His apprehension was suspended for the moment; whatever else she might be, she *was* a genius. This was what Ginny had intuited. She had responded to the honest artist in Darsen . . . the work was no less than magnificent. Manilla was good, yes, but young. These were masterworks. Oh poor babies, this was becoming increasingly complicated. His hard line was beginning to waver.

"So David, you're an artist, tell me . . ." Darsen moved in close, close enough for her breath to settle over him like a veil.

There was no heat, only cold. Pure, even as the scent of the wine was pure. He stepped away, closer to the paintings. "They're amazing — this seems to be an entirely new school of work. The color, what you do with color —"

Then he heard it.

Low, like a far off nest of insects, but slowly the whine grew. He turned but there was only Darsen, swathed in black satin and ruby.

"There aren't any, uh, bees in here, are there? I'm allergic to them and sometimes these old warehouses . . ."

"No David, no bees."

Then he heard the birds. Not exactly birdsong, but very close; strange to be inside with them, almost repulsive. Alien.

"An aviary? Come on, you can't tell me you don't keep birds." David smiled, carefully.

"Nothing, David. Simply the plants — and us. Maybe the wine was a little strong?" Darsen moved in front of the largest canvas.

To steady himself, David pulled the lens cap off his camera and popped the trigger.

"No!" It was a hiss.

He didn't stop, his head was beginning to spin.

"Not me, fool — only the paintings! Stop!" Darsen's eyes narrowed. For a moment it seemed as if light came from them, intense enough to make David freeze mid-shot.

159

"I always do this, candids of the artist first — it's my trademark, my signature," David whispered, trying to remain upright.

"Not of me! You'll have to forgo that dubious pleasure, my friend, or we terminate this contract immediately!" She was gone out of the camera's reach.

David tried to focus his eyes, scoping out the enormous space. "Hey, Darsen, we don't have a contract yet. I'm no lackey, lady. I choose my clients — they don't choose me!" His head was swimming. The colors of the room were making him mildly nauseated. It was obvious the plan was falling apart. She had too many games. She saw the plot, had to — now it was time to split!

"I am very disappointed, David. I had hoped this might become more than simple work — we might actually end as friends. That would be important to Virginia. However, if you are going to be so rigid —" She did not step from the pooled light.

"My dear spiderwoman, I'm no little fly — and by the way, this wine sucks, I think it's gone off. If this weren't already a grade-B movie I'd accuse you of poisoning me!" David swayed toward the elevator, not sure he'd make it intact. The air seemed to thicken around him, to grow alive. Something in it was moving, moving like ether, soothing but also killing him. He had to get outside!

Darsen followed, always in the shadows. Only her voice and the ruby glow of her eyes allowed him to place her. Jesus, her eyes! Like some jungle cat — Oh God — he needed the street. Unwilling to turn his back on her, he edged to the cage of the elevator and slipped in. He sighed as it swung shut and the perfectly oiled machinery lowered him. The fog in the street hit him full-face. His head felt full of opium fumes, like the time in Bangladesh; out of sync, hallucinating, some rubbery bones.

Christ, he hoped the campus cops wouldn't pick him up . . . Who knew what she had put into the damned wine?

David didn't notice the shadow emerge from the loft. He didn't notice the slow stalk. He was laughing. He clutched the camera bag close. At the very least he'd have some good shots to share with his set designer buddies!

Darsen followed easily. The night was her glory. No clues. Ginny would believe David had done what others had consistently done — vanished from her. It would add fuel to the fire Darsen was building around Manilla, too. No one could be trusted. Not David, not her lover — only Darsen. Darsen understood. Darsen was capable of promising absolute faithfulness. Darsen's long teeth were exposed as she smiled. Yes — unending faithfulness . . .

David fumbled with the keys. Like a damned co-ed. Jesus! The kids at the end of the street had shot out the lights again. Not even fucking Halloween yet. His fingers were numb. The bitch had drugged him, no doubt! Should he call the paramedics? Oh

God, having his stomach pumped was not something he cared to repeat in this life! Where the hell was the frigging key?

Her shadow moved on the lawn, mingling with the shadows of all night-growing things. Silently, she moved in for the strike.

She would let him know, oh yes, take him slowly, allow him to understand exactly what and who was doing this to him. He would pay for his pathetic game, pay for his paltry judgments. Her only hesitation was that he might have succeeded in alerting Manilla . . . Her plan could be suspended if the young dark one knew. Well, she would deal with that later. Now, she ached in each cold vein. She was throbbing with the promise of voluptuous kill. Afterward, she would destroy the film, the camera he had violated her with — shrivel them to elemental carbon and leave them at the bottom of Cayuga Lake. Darsen tore into the light behind him as he opened his door.

The dog leapt past David and out. David screamed. Shit! Shit! This was all he needed now, the standard poodle digging up the neighbors' yard or running around Collegetown! Shit! Fifty bucks if the cops caught it!

He heard the dog growling. Then it was off, chasing something. He hoped to God it wasn't someone who lived on his street. He'd be smacked with a lawsuit sure as hell. He whistled. The dog didn't come back. His head was too watery to go out looking. He'd had enough. He'd risk the ticket. Shit, shit, shit, what a bloody night!

* * * * *

162

The steps were light, sneakered.

Before she could prevent the key from slipping into her lock, Manilla was there. Ginny noticed the orchids were beginning to reek, to smell of death.

"Let me explain, please." She gestured lamely. "It was Darsen, I won't lie to you, but it's just her way of . . ."

Manilla didn't let Ginny get close enough to touch . . .

The night was as cloying as the flowers. Orchids! When had she ever been able to buy orchids? How could she compete? That Ginny was used to extraordinary gifts had always worried Manilla, an oblique threat that someday Ginny would wake up to the missing luxuries, notice that it had been too hard for too long. With Darsen's arrival, it had come to pass.

Ithaca was a bad dream. College towns were like distorted mirrors, everyone self-absorbed, warped, untouched by the outside. She had to get Ginny out of there. She felt the goosebumps rise on her arms. Ginny was being stalked by some huge jungle animal. Darsen wasn't human. Something wild clung to her — even her choice of flowers. Manilla hated that Ginny lived across from the woman. Darsen in her lair, painting, panting, waiting for Ginny to be alone . . . Like a big cat, half-asleep on the limb of a tree, napping until a victim passed beneath her. Well, Manilla wouldn't be caught. It was Darsen's turn to be hunted.

Manilla ran her fingers through her short curls, shaking out the fear, the terror. The anger had dissolved in the night air. She coldly knew what had to be done. Ginny wasn't a prize in some game show. Manilla would wait. If there came a time when Ginny or their relationship was in real danger, well, just let Darsen try to pounce!

Now she must go back, apologize for the fight, for running. Ginny would understand. Ginny knew her moods, her need to run until things came clear. Others had tried to corner her but Ginny gave space. In that space, Manilla could return. Ginny deserved the same gift, now.

Who had ever known her so well? Ginny made her strong — they made each other strong. They had been each other's family.

As she stood under the streetlight, Manilla realized that if Ginny honestly chose Darsen, she would let her go. She would honor an honest choice. Yes, she would honor it and continue to love Ginny.

When she got back to the loft there were lights. It was like finding a campfire after being lost in the woods. Ginny had brought her in from the dark. Manilla quickened her pace. Her heart beat out the staccato of Ginny's name . . . almost there, almost there — Then she stopped.

Something tall and dark moved across the street. Like a shadow light and quick, but no shadow. Before she saw the face, she knew. Something too sweet in the air, dense; then the sudden drop in temperature. Enough to register a slow shiver, enough to make one draw in one's arms and protect the body — Manilla recognized all of it. Darsen.

The shadow stopped in front of the loft door. It filled in, grew firm, took on human form. Manilla wanted to rub her eyes like a child waking from a nightmare — to make it go away. She tried to call out to warn Ginny, but she realized she couldn't speak.

She moved off, her feet scraping slightly as she pushed into an alley. She watched the golden rectangle of light spill from the loft's entrance onto the wet macadam. She heard her lover's voice. Then, Darsen turned. She turned and looked directly into the alley at Manilla.

It was as if Darsen's eyes pulled all the light from the street. Then a flash of teeth, the wicked smile. Before Manilla could recover, the door shut, the light broke. Darsen was inside.

The fatigue was overpowering. No more fight. No playtime, now. Better to get to Weston, leave, leave while there was a chance to get back. Nothing left inside her, not even the fear. Manilla turned down the alley and out toward the highway, beyond the lake.

Only the woods were familiar. Manilla picked her way like a night-living thing through the trees. They were her sentinels, protecting and hiding her. She couldn't let anyone see her this emptied out.

One of the townies had picked her up and given her a ride all the way back. She needed the forest. The dorms seem sinister, the campus insidious. Damn, why was she always on the outside, always so different?

The chill around Ithaca was lost by the time she got to Aura. She walked into the woods, comfortable for the first time in weeks. She made for the waterfall near the edge of campus. She could be quiet there, just let it all wash with the water. Holy place, Indian place. Maybe that was the key — she'd somehow become estranged from her tribe, was forever trying to find her way back . . .

A hand covered her mouth. Another arm pulled her tight against a pine tree. She stamped down hard, remembering the kneecap self-defense she'd been taught. The move had been telegraphed and the other body pulled her at an even tighter angle. Her heart screamed for release. The dark narrowed, a tunnel around her vision, please God, the Catholic cry rising in her, then, in her hair, her ear, soft breath, cool talk:

"If you don't scream, I'll let you go. I didn't mean to frighten you. I knew if I called out of the dark you'd be terrified. It's dangerous up here at night, Manilla . . . all right?"

Manilla felt the light coming back at the edges of her vision. Her heart calmed. The familiar voice was lovely in its familiarity. The hand came away from her lips.

"Professor Slater!"

"What are you doing here this time of night?" The woman knelt on the pine needles, close to Manilla.

"I should ask you! I just came in from Ithaca . . . bad night . . . with Ginny. Couldn't face the dorm. I come here a lot, must to think. This is the first time I've ever met anyone, though. You really scared me!"

"I didn't mean to." The woman's voice softened. "Sometimes I like to walk — but it's dangerous for a young woman to be out all alone, Manilla."

Manilla hugged her knees to her chest. "But it's okay for you, huh? Come on, this is Aura, nothing happens here, except maybe to animals."

"You know, you don't have to come up here. If you need to talk, you know where I live. I thought we settled that a few nights ago. We seem to hold a lot of secrets for each other." The woman touched Manilla's arm.

Manilla saw the flash of a ring in the moonlight. The small ruby flashed blood-red.

Something deep and hidden broke inside her at the sight of the ring. Manilla leaned back against the tree. Beginning with the start of school this fall, she began telling Slater everything.

As Slater listened she tried to check her excitement. "Manilla, go over everything you remember about this woman Darsen. Carefully, completely, please."

"Do you think you know her? I don't get it, Professor." Manilla had heard the edge in Slater's voice. The feeling of almost remembering, of deja vu, was maddening now. What was it that struck so deeply, why couldn't she figure it out?

"I'll explain everything to you. It's finally time." Slater stood up, her back to the forest and then she told:

Cold steel at a throat; ice against soft, inner flesh; a razor at a nipple; glaciers vast and bone-white;

alien; death; everything that Darsen was. It was enough.

This time there was no need for a probe. Manilla's heart was ready, the seeds had been planted, the images sprouted full. She believed, believed and knew it to be the truth.

"Will you help me?" Slater took Manilla's hand, pressed it hard.

"Yes."

"Look love," David said, "I don't expect you to believe a word of it, I'm not in the same place you've been in lately so I've mailed you some copies. I would hand deliver them but I've got to be out of here first thing. I've got an assignment for 'ArtUs' — but we'll talk about it later. I just called to tell you, well, be careful. What happens between you and Manilla is between you and Manilla — my first investment is you, Ginny. I could live if you broke up with the little dyke — much as I love her — the Good Fairy I'm not — but seriously, I want you to hold off making any rash decisions till I get back next week. There's something about that witch across the street from you — well, I can't prove anything, not just yet, but there's something very, very strange. Just take a look at the pictures I've sent. At the very least she's a man-hater. Now don't laugh — be careful, toots. She's big, big trouble. I have a sneaking suspicion she's into voodoo and Black Mass stuff — Ginny, I am serious! Well, we'll continue this later — just stay away from her till I get back. Promise me — I love you, kiddo." David hung up.

168

The bath had been running throughout the call. The studio smelled of lilies of the valley. Puffs of steam floated from the bathroom and into the living room.

"Someday I need to get this entire place on film," David mumbled, picking up his champagne flute on the way to the tub. He flipped on the stereo, flooding the place with Bach.

As he eased into the water he did not notice the change of light. Soft and steamy at first, then suddenly cold, very cold . . . It settled all around him.

Ginny hung up. Darsen had slipped away the minute she heard it was David. Ginny closed her eyes. A dull ache was living there, pounding out everything but its own life. Why couldn't anything be the way she wanted it? Was life supposed to be confusing? Darsen was unlike anyone she had ever known — Darsen completed her. Manilla complemented her but Darsen completed her. She loved Manilla — no doubt — and with Darsen, well, not so much love as something deeper and incredibly exciting.

Like the time after her father left them in Spain to go to Africa. At the fortress tower she was touring she had slipped away from the guide and the Secret Service men into a closed-off room. She knew she was not supposed to be there, but the door was unlocked and something inside compelled her.

Carefully she shut the door behind her, clothing herself in the musty air. No sounds, not even rats. She watched the gray light filter down, flirting with the walls. She allowed it all to play over her, to take control. Something electric ran across her exposed skin, under her clothes, deeper. She felt every hair on her body stand and pay homage to the current, the spirit of the room. Ginny, Ginny, as if some monster/beauty called out to her; Ginny — Oh, if anyone had been in the room with her at that moment she would have fallen upon them, taking them even as she wanted to be taken. But there was no one save for herself and it was not enough. So, instead, she had extended her hands like some trapped bird and raced round and round the tower.

Footsteps broke the reverie. Tourists. The power retreated. She froze, shook herself sane, stopped only long enough to rearrange her loosed hair, and then quickly slipped back to her family. No one noticed her return; but in those days, there had never been anyone to look very closely; never anyone until Manilla.

Manilla.

Manilla's touch was not maddening, not confusing — it warmed her, made her ache. Manilla didn't fill her with wildness. No — the passion was deep, exciting, but safe; it was home. She had to see Manilla, could not make this decision without seeing Manilla and telling her everything truthfully about Darsen.

The pain behind her eyes was almost blinding. It increased as she searched for her keys. As if trying to prevent her from escaping, her head pounded, her eyes beginning to tear with the unrelenting pain.

Something sickening was in the studio with her; invisible little devil, tormenting her, wanting her to stay, play with the pain of it, get to know its perverse pleasure. Ginny heard voices.

My God, was she having a breakdown like her mother?

She stumbled against the couch, knocking pillows to the floor. The key ring was lying there, almost too brilliant to touch. She grabbed for it, feeling it sear her palm, knowing it was impossible but also knowing the reality of the devil pain. She could get out, she could get out . . . Had to hold on to the certainty of that . . . Too terrified to look at her scalding flesh, she pressed the keys more tightly, trying to block out the hissing burn, the smell of blistered flesh.

Her mind was stretching — she would not allow it to snap. She heaved open the studio doors and plunged into the street. The VW waited for her, out front; good horse. Yes, she moved to it, got inside, sat, sat and waited. The pain in her hand began to vanish. Still, she could not look.

Wiping at the remaining tears, she pushed the car into gear, started off.

The housecleaner picked up the note in the mailbox. The instructions were different from the usual routine. The guy was going away for a while, still wanted the place cleaned, though. Geez. Must be nice to afford a cleaning lady when you weren't even home to mess up the place . . .

She opened the door. Dog was gone, must be at a kennel. She missed the thing — big, dumb animal, but nice. The smell of lilies hit her full — the house reeked! God help the woman he got close to.

She went around opening windows, trying to air the place out. Fresh air, best smell she knew.

She moved from the kitchen to the bathroom. The guy was neat but when it came to bathrooms all guys were pigs — she had the sons to prove it.

She leaned over heavily and nearly heaved into the tub.

Some kind of reddish scum floated on the top of a half-filled bathtub. Soap mixed in oily flakes with the rust-colored mold. Looked like he killed a rat there. It made her flesh crawl.

Well, no way around it. The tub was the old-fashioned, antiquey kind, half as big as the room, with claw feet and a rubber stopper. She put on her rubber gloves and rolled up her sleeves, trying not to gag as she reached in to pull the plug. Her knuckles brushed against something hard and smooth, about the size of an apple, at the bottom of the tub. She moved back, shaken. What the hell? Using her toilet brush she tried to push some of the floating film away to see below the surface. Maybe a rat did die in the water. How long had the guy been gone?

She couldn't tell with the crud floating around. At least the thing at the bottom didn't move. Ugh. She reached in gingerly and pulled the plug out fast. The water was motionless and then with a great heaving gurgle, started to suck down the drain. It was slow going. Finally, before she finished half of her cigarette, the water wound down the black hole with a belch. She sprayed down the sides of the tub and washed the lump at the bottom with scalding water.

Surprise surprise surprise! Some kind of big maroonish stone sat like a dead, red turtle near the drain. What the hell was that doing in the tub? They guy had money, but was he hiding smuggled jewels into the country, hiding them in his bath? Weird, very, very weird.

She scrubbed around the thing, cleaned out the guck, finished the rest of the room. She closed the door behind her, still puzzled. On second thought, the guy had left the stone underwater . . . who knew why? Maybe she should do the same. She rammed the plug back into the hole, ran the water to its original level, turned it off and backed out. Leastways now it was clean in there . . . and that was something . . .

The Boathouse, weather-proofed to protect the delicate craft it housed, was deserted. Manilla took Ginny's hand lightly and pushed open the door. Sunlight splashed on the keels of the sailboats. Outside, the rowboats bobbed and banged against the dock pylons. It was warm; the scents of crisp leaves, new canvas and clean wood rose around them, dust motes danced in the streaming light. Essential Weston: for Ginny and Manilla this was where it had started. Parties in early spring. In the heat of the Boathouse dancefloor, Ginny had found Manilla.

They had never danced together, no. Ginny, golden dancer, danced alone. Manilla had cruised blatantly. She had been in thrall to the older student. Ginny had smelled of hyacinth.

Today, back in the house, Ginny still carried the scent. She spread the old quilt that had covered Manilla's bed since childhood. Soft colors, muted from a hundred washings, mixed with the spring hues surrounding them. Even their summer tans had faded to light gold.

Ginny's hair was like wild grass at the edge of the fields, all tawny golds and yellowed browns. Manilla's resembled the mown cornfields bordering the campus — shorn close but soft, dark, earthy. Ginny reached out and pulled Manilla down toward the quilt.

"Why can't it always be this simple, this lovely?" Ginny whispered into her lover's neck.

"It can be," Manilla answered, tingling as Ginny's tongue slid into her ear, exploring deeply.

"I have always loved you, Manilla — no matter what you worry about. I just get confused. Just know, it's always been you, will always be you." Ginny bit softly at Manilla's exposed neck, her hands softly tracing the strong muscles of her back.

"Sometimes it's so hard . . . I try not to worry, but this Darsen now, something, something wrong about her, Gin. I promised not to say more till the whole thing clears, but there's someone here who knows her. It sounds silly but I'm really scared for you, scared about what this woman is doing to us." Manilla gently pushed away.

Ginny said stubbornly, "I don't want to know about Darsen or Weston or what this other person knows. Darsen is a famous painter — I'm sure a lot of people know about her. Frankly, Manilla, I'm surprised you don't at least know her work. You should see it — you'd be impressed. She might even help you, you know. She wants to meet you — don't look at me like that! She's just my friend, babe, just reminds me of my past, the good parts. I don't want to lose that now. I don't want to fight you about that, either — we spent the whole day processing this and it's enough! No more talking, all right honey? No more. It's you I want, just for you to be with me, to love me . . ." Ginny rolled on top of Manilla playfully.

"But Gin, Professor Slater is —" Manilla's words were blotted out by Ginny's mouth, Ginny's hands.

They did not hear the geese shouting warnings from across the lake.

Slater was alone. The science building was quiet, not a single light buzzed in the entire building. Only the blurp and boil of the salt water tank broke the silence.

She moved quickly, choosing her shadow-speed, time was dear. She hit the bolted doors to the primate room loudly enough for the monkeys to cry out in fear. No one else would hear. Students were in dorms early these nights as rumors floated up and down the lake: missing people, dead animals.

Slater did not turn on the lights. Unnecessary. The animals quieted. They knew her. The game had been played out before. They did not resist. It was merely their fate — whichever creature fell to her blade. They watched, only the withdrawn bodies, the whites of their eyes betraying emotion.

She came to the cage of the largest. Her mind moved on a wave washing over the primal forest of thought, probing. This time, no blood, this time only memory. Humans had not yet made the connection but would ultimately. Animal minds were different —

crude by human standards — and yet, they had mastered an elemental probe of their own. Sea mammals were the most astute at its use, their abilities developed enough to pass on traditions from generations before, to travel thousands of miles in an instant, reaching particular individuals half a hemisphere away.

When she had first realized this side-power, the knowledge had been thrilling. It was the one bit of positive fall-out from Darsen; then she realized that to expose the knowledge to the scientific community would bring immediate attention to herself. If she was to succeed in tracking the Monster down, she had to exist in the light at the edge of the science community.

Her half-human — as yet, still human — self had cried countless nights with the futility of her new-found knowledge. It would be centuries before the human race came close to the power of the probe. Perhaps they would not exist long enough even for that. But the higher law was final; she could not reveal it. Her quest was paramount. It would die with her, she hoped; and with Darsen.

Tonight, as she moved among the monkeys, she pushed them to use their rude probings — to pick up guarded thoughts among other animals miles away. Even Darsen herself would not be free from their search. She would recognize Slater's probe immediately, but the animal signals were so constant and non-threatening, she would dismiss them. It was a solid chance.

The monkeys did not hate Slater for this. They held no capacity for that free-willed emotion. They did not like pain and responded to physical cruelty, but the probe was not painful. In fact, she touched their pleasure centers gently when she coursed through their minds. Carefully now, she sent the probe out like a telegram to the most mature animal. She let it be known that if it helped her it would receive fresh fruit in reward. The animals trusted the reward.

Slater felt the creature suddenly slump against its cage door, lids half-covered, eyes glazed. She felt her own mind pick up the images . . . and then the animal sat bolt upright, its eyes bright with terror.

An agonizing scream pierced the all-quiet lab. The monkey fell back, comatose, its pain center almost burned out.

Slater moved away from the cage, nauseated. The image had transferred intact. It ran like a black and white movie in her head. The vibration of Darsen's killings, her intents. The history with Manilla and Ginny. All of it now resonated through the animal to Slater. She was absolutely sure. What she had heard from Manilla and probed from Manilla had been colored by Manilla's interpretations, her emotions. What was now gleaned from the animal brain held no value judgments, no coloration. It was Darsen — she knew it. And now, Darsen must know for certain who she was — the animal's pain proved it. Darsen would be waiting for her to move . . .

Slater closed the lab doors, making certain the animals were again quiet. She did what she could for the animal that had given part of its mind for her . . . but it could not be much. She left them all in deep sleep.

In the corridor the air was inert; the smell of formaldehyde steeped into the very walls. It was an evil odor. She hated everything that pretended to suspend decay. Death was final, somehow beautiful in its finality. It was not decay — only ultimate release — into the arms of Good or Evil, an end to the limits of the planet, this life. Paltry attempts at keeping the husk intact were pathetic. They sickened her.

She moved through the corridor and thought about Darsen. She had been seen as weak in Darsen's view, with no taste for killing. This is what separated her from Darsen's kind.

Finally, the last duel. The cycle must stop; Darsen would take Ginny if it didn't. Darsen needed another lover. Too many years had passed, the hunger for connection must be weakening her, even as it was Slater. Ginny would be pressed into making the pact. Ginny would become a vampire.

Two times in the past Slater had almost succumbed. She had fought it and barely won. The loneliness could be battled, but the passion could not. Finally Ginny would be given the ultimate choice: all that was still human in her would be erased by the act of murder. If she did not kill a human she would remain forever trapped in a half-life, even as Slater herself, and Darsen would either abandon her or kill her.

What happened in their death? Was their soul intact? Would there be another existence? She didn't know. And what if she managed to kill Darsen — would that then fulfill the vow, would she herself become a full vampire? If that were true, then all the myths and magic, all the stories and insanity held court. There indeed were demons and there was truly a dark place. To die a vampire was to dwell in that kingdom forever . . .

The moon was achingly full as she came out of the science hall. Time to find Manilla. Time to prepare the trap.

"Where's Ginny?" Slater let Manilla inside but not before glancing up and down the street.

"Collegetown, the loft. At least that's where she said she'd be when we spoke this afternoon — why?" Manilla stepped inside the Professor's house. "Why did you need to see me tonight?"

"Sit down, please. There are some things you must know before we set out. Complicated, unbelievable things." Slater walked to the living room, motioning for Manilla to follow. Manilla felt very cold.

"The other night, in the woods, you came to understand about Darsen and her evil in a concentrated way — a way that is not communication as you've known it." Slater was picking her words carefully, standing over the seated young woman.

"You told me . . ." Manilla was confused, trying to remember the words, remembering only images, and a feeling of terror . . .

"Manilla!"

The voice commanded attention inside her head. Unlike Slater's speaking voice, this voice was demanding.

Manilla looked at Slater questioningly. Slater's eyes had changed. For an instant the same dread cold she had felt on her first encounter with Darsen seeped inside.

"Manilla!" Again the voice commanded her silence.

Slater was in front of her, directly — and then the voice and the woman were across the room. Another blink — they were in the front foyer by the door where moments before Manilla had entered. Another second and Slater was before her again — gazing deeply into Manilla, the eyes gone blood red . . .

"I am who I am, not like Darsen, but not unlike her, either. Don't close me out with your fear — listen now! Because I can see you, you have been shown the truth. You must pay close, close attention; you will feel the truth if you allow it. You must have more than simple understanding of what is to come, you must believe! If you believe, there is a chance. Do not be afraid, my sweet friend . . ."

Slater moved toward Manilla slowly. Bending down, she lifted her upper lip, exposing a canine both longer and sharper than any human tooth Manilla had ever seen. On the opposite side, another, perfectly matched.

Manilla's mind recoiled. The talk of Darsen, the danger she had felt when Darsen was discussed, even the night at the waterfall when she had spoken of Ginny, and Slater shared some of the evil Darsen was capable of — nothing had seemed unreal then. It was all plausible — mysterious but possible. Now, this nightmare in front of her with the burning eyes and fangs . . .

But this was upstate New York. Modern times. Weston College. What the hell?

"Exactly," spoke the voice that was not Slater's voice, the voice in her mind. "And why is this more fantastic than that which has come before, that which is accepted as reality? Think of the blood that has been spilled in these hills — genocide, human immolations, incest, suicide, rape. Oh, there are many monsters afoot on the planet, Manilla, and all of them have at one time been touched or created by Darsen's tribe. More horror than we can comprehend surrounds us each day. Where do you think the myths came from? There are angels, yes, and then there are others, whether you believe it or not. And all the exorcisms and purges in the world will not stop them. It goes on child, it goes on!"

Manilla's mind screamed back, trying to hold on to some kind of logic in the madness now revealed. "Why haven't you hurt me — why haven't you made me like you, like Darsen? It would have been so easy."

The voice roared, "Yes, it would have been so easy. There were moments, when you first came to me after years of loneliness, of burning crushing my spirit. If I had taken you then I would truly have become like Darsen. No. I will not allow it!"

Manilla was numbed. The truth overwhelmed her, but it was the truth. She felt it. Even seeing Slater fully uncovered, without disguise, did not make it more real. She knew the truth.

"In the jungle I allowed it to happen because I was convinced we were in a New Garden — we were going to be Eve's daughters. I tell you this because I know what Ginny sees. You must never blame her for it. There is no way someone can refuse Darsen once

181

she has been chosen. Darsen reads all that you lack, she reads it from your own mind. She then makes known that she can fulfill those needs, make whole that which was not. She is the promise and the artifice of love, human love. Ginny doesn't see Darsen as we do. She experiences Darsen the way Darsen allows. I know — for she once held me in the same way. You must love Ginny harder, you must fight for Ginny. All that may be left is what you can reach — the rest is useless ash."

"But you escaped, you resisted. I know Ginny," Manilla sobbed, "I know she'll fight for herself."

"You can't know her as completely as Darsen does, Manilla; even Ginny may be blind to that which Darsen sees inside. Often, in the jungle, Darsen would enter my actual dreams, living them with me, then later speak as if the dream had taken place. I never knew what was real and what had been dreamed. She could follow me anywhere. In my realization of that, there was surprising relief. We are so often taught feelings of lack, of incompletion as people — finally there was someone who wanted me totally, so much that all I was or dreamed was taken over. Ginny is like this. Darsen takes only those with that kind of absolute need. Perhaps that is why she did not choose you. Your needs are different. Ginny is less resilient, more open. If she were not, Darsen would have simply killed her by now. Once one of Darsen's kind has revealed herself there are few choices." Slater's voice stopped.

"No!" Manilla felt the horror.

"The power she promises is the final seduction. She offers that which she displays. There is a universe you pass through, we all pass through daily, but do not even dream exists. All will be revealed through her! Manilla, she can teach you to come face to face with your Creator!"

"You can't believe . . ." Manilla trembled.

"Yes, I do believe! I was witness to it — there are no words that will suffice — the images would tear your mind open if I tried to place them there. You see, Darsen, her kind, they were the first — they are evil incarnate!"

"And what of you?" Manilla whispered, weak with fear.

"Half-demon ha! Such irony in that! But the potential is always present — will be till my own end. Only after Darsen gave me the gifts did she mention the final sacrament; when I would not drink of the living flesh then she tried to kill me. In your memory now, go back to the jungle — the fire. Allow my probe to rekindle it. You see my escape — Darsen's retreat — she thought me destroyed and went on without a thought, did not require another lover until now."

Slater stared fixedly at Manilla. "She can't have Ginny fully until I am dead — perhaps this one fact has kept Ginny safe. For Darsen knows, finally, that I am still alive, and tracking her. If Darsen attempts to finalize the act with Ginny, Ginny will perish. The power cannot be passed on unless it is pure. Darsen must kill me first, to purify her gift. It is her one vow. Because you were once Ginny's love, she must also destroy you — we are marked. I have told you all of this because of that fact. Darsen is the Dark One, Manilla. To follow her is to lose your soul."

There was silence. On the distant lake shore a soft, pink light rose. The room was frigid.

Manilla looked up into the ruby eyes.

Slater murmured, "We must decide on a plan. Nothing complicated — too easy to stumble over complications. We must decide something so obvious that Darsen will dismiss it. This is her vulnerable time, too, so much is in motion for the seduction. She must carefully balance the energy. She won't stray far from her goal though she will be distracted by knowing I'm alive. It's our one advantage. Her pride will be a hindrance — it always has been. Now, some facts, Ginny's schedules, people she knows . . ."

Outside, the light in the eastern sky grew rainbowed. The gold rose and broke into morning. Leaves blew in circles, playful, fulfilled in their autumn promise. Only the geese at the edge of the freezing water felt the difference. The subtle, sudden drop in temperature, the dryness in the air — the geese knew. There was a new presence among them and it was very, very cold . . .

"You're lying!" Ginny threw the juice glass into the sink, shattering it. "If it's true why don't I have bat wings and fangs by now? Are you doing drugs again? I beg you to just trust me, not to be crazy jealous and you go off the deep end! You are severely twisted, Manilla!"

"When have I ever lied to you? I know what this sounds like — but Ginny, so help me, it's God's truth! David tried to warn us." Manilla stood inside the door.

"David, right, where is the slug when I need him? Tells me to be careful of big, bad Darsen, says he's

sending this pack of pictures which will prove all . . .
Well I got those photos and you know what? Zip.
Yeah, just some gorgeous shots of Darsen's paintings
— maybe he should submit them to *Art in America.*
Or would you prefer that *Vampires United* got a set?
Dammit Manilla, I think you both should see a
shrink! It's Weston and the lunatics there — they're
warping you. Nothing is happening between Darsen
and me. I love you, Goddammit, why isn't that ever
enough?" Ginny burst into tears, turning away.

"I'm leaving now. I love you — and because I do,
I'm going. I'll be close if you need me. You have to
trust too, Gin. I don't know why this has happened
to us, or how many other people are involved, but it
has to stop." Fighting her own tears, Manilla walked
out.

The street was full of college traffic. Bikes
whizzed by, cars honked, people jogged all the way up
the hill to Cornell. Bright jackets and down vests
were emblems against fear.

How ancient was this disease? Who carried the
germ inside? Would she ever be able to be in a crowd
again without wondering about the horror? Manilla
tucked her hands into her pockets and walked
downtown. If there were only a God — a God could
stop it. If there weren't, well, maybe a vampire was
as good as anything else . . .

Ginny remained by the sink. She closed her eyes,
forcing the tears to stop, her hands raw from
clutching the metal counter edge. She drank some
water but the taste was so greasy she spat it out.

Turning, she faced her reflection in the kitchen mirror. The morning light had changed. It spread through the loft and caught her eyes. For the first time, Ginny saw for herself the ruby color creeping in . . .

Darsen was above Ginny. Sweat bathed her, made her moist and maddened with its sting. She could wait no longer, indeed, had waited for years. Everything was risked now in the moment of this single act. She would be complete. No one would ever be able to hurt her again. She cupped the back of the elegant head and brought it down, down.

Ginny felt her moisture rise, knew the cold, almost frozen breath of Darsen. She smelled the womanscent of her — the slow ache, the heavy throbbing.

A single, instantaneous movement, all pain and swift pleasure, more pleasure than anyone had dared breathe to her; she knew the parting of her lips, down to her wet center, knew the piercing, almost cruel plunge, but so much joy! She was close, so close now . . .

"Darsen!"

The scream brought Darsen up, snarling.

"Darsen, no!"

Darsen whirled around, knocking the candles by the bed onto the floor in one smoking, furious gesture.

The door slammed open. Ginny tried to call out. Everything seemed freeze-framed, her body still blazing, her mind filled with that heat; she could neither scream nor breathe.

"I thought you were dead!" The voice was Darsen's but unlike Darsen — almost animal. Ginny recoiled from the sound.

"You knew I was alive! No more lies! You plotted to kill me tonight, I know it! I was here before you — don't try to cloud your mind! Your arrogance will be your last mistake!"

Slater was across the room and on top of the vampire. The hiss and snarl of animals locked in deadly battle filled the room.

Fire from the spilled candles began to light the bedclothes. Ginny could not move. Fast, all of it, too fast.

Smoke began to boil around them. They moved like monstrous shadows through it, then, like shadows, seemed to become part of the smoke. Cries, jungle sounds, all in the minds of those in the loft — the fire's roar a strange music.

Ginny could do nothing. The smoke was a shroud and she was suffocating beneath it. The fire was so close she could feel her skin begin to blister.

Then, someone had her. It might have been Darsen. She was half-dragged, half-carried across the warping floor. Down, down through the cracking wood and tile, the sprinklers finally bursting open, the evil hiss of water on flame baptizing them as they descended the stairs.

The ash clung in gray disguise; Ginny knew nothing but the scrape of the cement steps against her ankles and the sudden blast of night air filling her smoke-bitten lungs.

Sirens wailed around the corner. New screams, human. Throngs of students, neighbors, filling the street and Ginny repeating over and over that there were still people up in the loft . . . still . . . still . . . Then they carried her away . . .

Manilla pushed past the crowd. She clawed through the billowing smoke. Sparks danced over her head. The heat drove her back but she fought it, fueled by the absolute need to get to Slater. She had to help the woman who had saved their lives. Slater was dying up in the inferno, either by Darsen's fangs or the flames themselves.

The fire licked down, scorching her face, singeing her hair, her eyebrows almost burned off. The jacket on Manilla's back burst into flame as she tore up the stairs. Manilla flung it aside, not stopping for a moment. The horror of the noise at the top of the stairs drove even the fear of fire from her. Inhuman screams, the metallic sound of clicking fangs as they slashed and missed mid-air, this was the jungle's chorus of death, huge predators locked in mortal combat.

Manilla yelled for Slater; if Slater could only reach her there was a way out. The bathroom window; the fire hadn't reached there! But Slater didn't answer. Only the terrifying sounds of burning and the thundering battle echoed.

Suddenly Darsen appeared — but this was a transformed Darsen — a monster of unbelievable outline, with clacking fangs and huge leathery wings which beat at the scalding air. Manilla strained to see Slater through the fanned smoke but was blasted aside as the heat intensified. She held up her fists, a futile attempt to block the sounds of screaming.

A deafening explosion sprayed shards of glass like shrapnel thought the ruptured studio. Manilla was thrown to the floor as an enormous fireball hurtled over, screamingly alive, shrieking even as it burst out into the writhing night above the heads of the throng in the street below.

An arm, solid, pushed Manilla toward the bathroom. The door slammed behind them, against the flames. The window to the fire escape was broken. Manilla gulped at the fresh air. Turning, she tried to wipe the blood from her seared eyes. Through the distortion she saw Slater! In the midst of the terror there remained Slater! But Slater was slipping away — Manilla felt it. Trying to hold on to her, to keep her alive, Manilla pressed the dying professor to her chest, pushing her toward her own heart, trying vainly to pump the energy that beat there into the fading woman . . .

Manilla sobbed, the sounds wracking through her burning throat, "Please don't leave me . . . don't go . . ."

"It's done . . . be glad . . . if only we, a long time ago, in the jungle . . . Might have been different, Manilla . . . maybe . . ."

The weight was gone, vanished, Manilla held only ashes and then these too moved up, mingling with the smoke, out, into the night. Manilla watched the sparking flight. Then, in her hand, something warm, heavy, hard; it was Slater's ruby ring. Manilla closed her eyes, slipped it on . . .

A firefighter met her on the fire escape, hauled her down, the building beginning to crumple in on itself even as they scrambled for the street. The ambulance waited. Ginny was on a stretcher, an oxygen mask held tightly to her face. Manilla was helped in beside her. She reached for Ginny's cold, cold hand . . .

The sheriff held out a familiar envelope. Manilla recognized the stationery immediately. He shook his head as he handed it to her. "It's addressed to you . . . don't think we'll need it for evidence. You were damned lucky, you and your friend. College kids and candles . . . fire marshall says it was just a freaky accident. Like a lot of freaky things this fall . . . dead animals . . . missing people, well, I suppose this won't answer any of my questions . . . damned lucky . . ." The sheriff moved off down the hall.

Manilla ran her fingers lightly over the envelope. She didn't have to read the note on the cream-colored paper. She wouldn't say a thing to the college about Slater's departure. Let them think what they wanted. Too much pressure, a sudden affair — or, like the sheriff had said, a freaky autumn. It didn't matter anymore what any of them thought.

Manilla reached for the matches in her pocket. Standing over the institutional ashcan she lit the edge of the paper, being very careful about the flames. Even she had to smile.

190

It was All Hallow's Eve.

The nurse shut the curtains that circled Ginny's bed. Ginny was scheduled to be released at noon, the next day. She had been given a sedative and tucked in — the more sleep she had, the better. It had been a hellish time for this lovely co-ed. The nurse shook her head.

The doctor smiled sympathetically, flipping through Ginny's chart. "Her father's that diplomat," he said.

"Yes, I know. We've been trying to contact the family. She doesn't seem worried about it — her only concern is that any information be shared . . . with her friend. You know, the little dark one with the funny name, down the hall, what is it . . . Manilla? That's right. She says Manilla is her family. We haven't argued, they're both over twenty-one."

"Mmmmm. Yes. Strange, this, though. Says there is a tiny puncture wound on the inside of the groin . . . Watch it, will you, for infection. Must have occurred as she was dragged out. Almost looks like an animal bite. Any dogs in that place? Too large for a rat . . . The things that can happen to people make me cringe! Ask her about it when she's awake, will you? Keep me posted on any changes."

They left the room. They switched the light off behind them.

A few of the publications of
THE NAIAD PRESS, INC.
P.O. Box 10543 ● Tallahassee, Florida 32302
Phone (904) 539-5965
Mail orders welcome. Please include 15% postage.

VIRAGO by Karen Marie Christa Minns. 208 pp. Darsen has
chosen Ginny.   ISBN 0-941483-56-8 $8.95

WILDERNESS TREK by Dorothy Tell. 160 pp. Six women on
vacation learning "new" skills.   ISBN 0-941483-60-6   8.95

MURDER BY THE BOOK by Pat Welch. 240 pp. A Helen
Black Mystery. First in a series.   ISBN 0-941483-59-2   8.95

BERRIGAN by Vicki P. McConnell. 176 pp. Youthful Lesbian–
romantic, idealistic Berrigan.   ISBN 0-941483-55-X   8.95

LESBIANS IN GERMANY by Lillian Faderman & B. Eriksson.
128 pp. Fiction, poetry, essays.   ISBN 0-941483-62-2   8.95

THE BEVERLY MALIBU by Katherine V. Forrest. 288 pp. A
Kate Delafield Mystery. 3rd in a series.   ISBN 0-941483-47-9   16.95

THERE'S SOMETHING I'VE BEEN MEANING TO TELL
YOU Ed. by Loralee MacPike. 288 pp. Gay men and lesbians
coming out to their children.   ISBN 0-941483-44-4   9.95
                                         ISBN 0-941483-54-1   16.95

LIFTING BELLY by Gertrude Stein. Ed. by Rebecca Mark. 104
pp. Erotic poetry.   ISBN 0-941483-51-7   8.95
                                         ISBN 0-941483-53-3   14.95

ROSE PENSKI by Roz Perry. 192 pp. Adult lovers in a long-term
relationship.   ISBN 0-941483-37-1   8.95

AFTER THE FIRE by Jane Rule. 256 pp. Warm, human novel
by this incomparable author.   ISBN 0-941483-45-2   8.95

SUE SLATE, PRIVATE EYE by Lee Lynch. 176 pp. The gay
folk of Peacock Alley are *all* cats.   ISBN 0-941483-52-5   8.95

CHRIS by Randy Salem. 224 pp. Golden oldie. Handsome Chris
and her adventures.   ISBN 0-941483-42-8   8.95

THREE WOMEN by March Hastings. 232 pp. Golden oldie. A
triangle among wealthy sophisticates.   ISBN 0-941483-43-6   8.95

RICE AND BEANS by Valeria Taylor. 232 pp. Love and
romance on poverty row.   ISBN 0-941483-41-X   8.95

PLEASURES by Robbi Sommers. 204 pp. Unprecedented
eroticism.   ISBN 0-941483-49-5   8.95

EDGEWISE by Camarin Grae. 372 pp. Spellbinding
adventure.   ISBN 0-941483-19-3   9.95

FATAL REUNION by Claire McNab. 216 pp. 2nd Det. Inspec.
Carol Ashton mystery.   ISBN 0-941483-40-1   8.95

KEEP TO ME STRANGER by Sarah Aldridge. 372 pp. Romance
set in a department store dynasty. ISBN 0-941483-38-X 9.95

HEARTSCAPE by Sue Gambill. 204 pp. American lesbian in
Portugal. ISBN 0-941483-33-9 8.95

IN THE BLOOD by Lauren Wright Douglas. 252 pp. Lesbian
science fiction adventure fantasy ISBN 0-941483-22-3 8.95

THE BEE'S KISS by Shirley Verel. 216 pp. Delicate, delicious
romance. ISBN 0-941483-36-3 8.95

RAGING MOTHER MOUNTAIN by Pat Emmerson. 264 pp.
Furosa Firechild's adventures in Wonderland. ISBN 0-941483-35-5 8.95

IN EVERY PORT by Karin Kallmaker. 228 pp. Jessica's sexy,
adventuresome travels. ISBN 0-941483-37-7 8.95

OF LOVE AND GLORY by Evelyn Kennedy. 192 pp. Exciting
WWII romance. ISBN 0-941483-32-0 8.95

CLICKING STONES by Nancy Tyler Glenn. 288 pp. Love
transcending time. ISBN 0-941483-31-2 8.95

SURVIVING SISTERS by Gail Pass. 252 pp. Powerful love
story. ISBN 0-941483-16-9 8.95

SOUTH OF THE LINE by Catherine Ennis. 216 pp. Civil War
adventure. ISBN 0-941483-29-0 8.95

WOMAN PLUS WOMAN by Dolores Klaich. 300 pp. Supurb
Lesbian overview. ISBN 0-941483-28-2 9.95

SLOW DANCING AT MISS POLLY'S by Sheila Ortiz Taylor.
96 pp. Lesbian Poetry ISBN 0-941483-30-4 7.95

DOUBLE DAUGHTER by Vicki P. McConnell. 216 pp. A Nyla
Wade Mystery, third in the series. ISBN 0-941483-26-6 8.95

HEAVY GILT by Delores Klaich. 192 pp. Lesbian detective/
disappearing homophobes/upper class gay society.

ISBN 0-941483-25-8 8.95

THE FINER GRAIN by Denise Ohio. 216 pp. Brilliant young
college lesbian novel. ISBN 0-941483-11-8 8.95

THE AMAZON TRAIL by Lee Lynch. 216 pp. Life, travel & lore
of famous lesbian author. ISBN 0-941483-27-4 8.95

HIGH CONTRAST by Jessie Lattimore. 264 pp. Women of the
Crystal Palace. ISBN 0-941483-17-7 8.95

OCTOBER OBSESSION by Meredith More. Josie's rich, secret
Lesbian life. ISBN 0-941483-18-5 8.95

LESBIAN CROSSROADS by Ruth Baetz. 276 pp. Contemporary
Lesbian lives. ISBN 0-941483-21-5 9.95

BEFORE STONEWALL: THE MAKING OF A GAY AND
LESBIAN COMMUNITY by Andrea Weiss & Greta Schiller.
96 pp., 25 illus. ISBN 0-941483-20-7 7.95

FOR KEEPS by Elisabeth Nonas. 144 pp. Contemporary novel about losing and finding love. ISBN 0-930044-71-1   7.95

TORCHLIGHT TO VALHALLA by Gale Wilhelm. 128 pp. Classic novel by a great Lesbian writer. ISBN 0-930044-68-1   7.95

LESBIAN NUNS: BREAKING SILENCE edited by Rosemary Curb and Nancy Manahan. 432 pp. Unprecedented autobiographies of religious life. ISBN 0-930044-62-2   9.95

THE SWASHBUCKLER by Lee Lynch. 288 pp. Colorful novel set in Greenwich Village in the sixties. ISBN 0-930044-66-5   8.95

MISFORTUNE'S FRIEND by Sarah Aldridge. 320 pp. Historical Lesbian novel set on two continents. ISBN 0-930044-67-3   7.95

A STUDIO OF ONE'S OWN by Ann Stokes. Edited by Dolores Klaich. 128 pp. Autobiography. ISBN 0-930044-64-9   7.95

SEX VARIANT WOMEN IN LITERATURE by Jeannette Howard Foster. 448 pp. Literary history. ISBN 0-930044-65-7   8.95

A HOT-EYED MODERATE by Jane Rule. 252 pp. Hard-hitting essays on gay life; writing; art. ISBN 0-930044-57-6   7.95

INLAND PASSAGE AND OTHER STORIES by Jane Rule. 288 pp. Wide-ranging new collection. ISBN 0-930044-56-8   7.95

WE TOO ARE DRIFTING by Gale Wilhelm. 128 pp. Timeless Lesbian novel, a masterpiece. ISBN 0-930044-61-4   6.95

AMATEUR CITY by Katherine V. Forrest. 224 pp. A Kate Delafield mystery. First in a series. ISBN 0-930044-55-X   7.95

THE SOPHIE HOROWITZ STORY by Sarah Schulman. 176 pp. Engaging novel of madcap intrigue. ISBN 0-930044-54-1   7.95

THE BURNTON WIDOWS by Vickie P. McConnell. 272 pp. A Nyla Wade mystery, second in the series. ISBN 0-930044-52-5   7.95

OLD DYKE TALES by Lee Lynch. 224 pp. Extraordinary stories of our diverse Lesbian lives. ISBN 0-930044-51-7   8.95

DAUGHTERS OF A CORAL DAWN by Katherine V. Forrest. 240 pp. Novel set in a Lesbian new world. ISBN 0-930044-50-9   7.95

THE PRICE OF SALT by Claire Morgan. 288 pp. A milestone novel, a beloved classic. ISBN 0-930044-49-5   8.95

AGAINST THE SEASON by Jane Rule. 224 pp. Luminous, complex novel of interrelationships. ISBN 0-930044-48-7   8.95

LOVERS IN THE PRESENT AFTERNOON by Kathleen Fleming. 288 pp. A novel about recovery and growth. ISBN 0-930044-46-0   8.95

TOOTHPICK HOUSE by Lee Lynch. 264 pp. Love between two Lesbians of different classes. ISBN 0-930044-45-2   7.95

MADAME AURORA by Sarah Aldridge. 256 pp. Historical novel featuring a charismatic "seer." ISBN 0-930044-44-4   7.95

CURIOUS WINE by Katherine V. Forrest. 176 pp. Passionate
Lesbian love story, a best-seller.   ISBN 0-930044-43-6   8.95

BLACK LESBIAN IN WHITE AMERICA by Anita Cornwell.
141 pp. Stories, essays, autobiography.   ISBN 0-930044-41-X   7.50

CONTRACT WITH THE WORLD by Jane Rule. 340 pp.
Powerful, panoramic novel of gay life.   ISBN 0-930044-28-2   9.95

MRS. PORTER'S LETTER by Vicki P. McConnell. 224 pp.
The first Nyla Wade mystery.   ISBN 0-930044-29-0   7.95

TO THE CLEVELAND STATION by Carol Anne Douglas.
192 pp. Interracial Lesbian love story.   ISBN 0-930044-27-4   6.95

THE NESTING PLACE by Sarah Aldridge. 224 pp. A
three-woman triangle—love conquers all!   ISBN 0-930044-26-6   7.95

THIS IS NOT FOR YOU by Jane Rule. 284 pp. A letter to a
beloved is also an intricate novel.   ISBN 0-930044-25-8   8.95

FAULTLINE by Sheila Ortiz Taylor. 140 pp. Warm, funny,
literate story of a startling family.   ISBN 0-930044-24-X   6.95

THE LESBIAN IN LITERATURE by Barbara Grier. 3d ed.
Foreword by Maida Tilchen. 240 pp. Comprehensive bibliography.
Literary ratings; rare photos.   ISBN 0-930044-23-1   7.95

ANNA'S COUNTRY by Elizabeth Lang. 208 pp. A woman
finds her Lesbian identity.   ISBN 0-930044-19-3   6.95

PRISM by Valerie Taylor. 158 pp. A love affair between two
women in their sixties.   ISBN 0-930044-18-5   6.95

BLACK LESBIANS: AN ANNOTATED BIBLIOGRAPHY
compiled by J. R. Roberts. Foreword by Barbara Smith. 112 pp.
Award-winning bibliography.   ISBN 0-930044-21-5   5.95

THE MARQUISE AND THE NOVICE by Victoria Ramstetter.
108 pp. A Lesbian Gothic novel.   ISBN 0-930044-16-9   6.95

OUTLANDER by Jane Rule. 207 pp. Short stories and essays
by one of our finest writers.   ISBN 0-930044-17-7   8.95

ALL TRUE LOVERS by Sarah Aldridge. 292 pp. Romantic
novel set in the 1930s and 1940s.   ISBN 0-930044-10-X   7.95

A WOMAN APPEARED TO ME by Renee Vivien. 65 pp. A
classic; translated by Jeannette H. Foster. ISBN 0-930044-06-1   5.00

CYTHEREA'S BREATH by Sarah Aldridge. 240 pp. Romantic
novel about women's entrance into medicine.
                                             ISBN 0-930044-02-9   6.95

TOTTIE by Sarah Aldridge. 181 pp. Lesbian romance in the
turmoil of the sixties.   ISBN 0-930044-01-0   6.95

THE LATECOMER by Sarah Aldridge. 107 pp. A delicate love
story.   ISBN 0-930044-00-2   6.95

ODD GIRL OUT by Ann Bannon. ISBN 0-930044-83-5 5.95
I AM A WOMAN by Ann Bannon. ISBN 0-930044-84-3 5.95
WOMEN IN THE SHADOWS by Ann Bannon.
ISBN 0-930044-85-1 5.95
JOURNEY TO A WOMAN by Ann Bannon.
ISBN 0-930044-86-X 5.95
BEEBO BRINKER by Ann Bannon. ISBN 0-930044-87-8 5.95
Legendary novels written in the fifties and sixties,
set in the gay mecca of Greenwich Village.

VOLUTE BOOKS

JOURNEY TO FULFILLMENT   Early classics by Valerie   3.95
A WORLD WITHOUT MEN   Taylor: The Erika Frohmann   3.95
RETURN TO LESBOS   series.   3.95

These are just a few of the many Naiad Press titles — we are the oldest and
largest lesbian/feminist publishing company in the world. Please request a
complete catalog. We offer personal service; we encourage and welcome
direct mail orders from individuals who have limited access to bookstores
carrying our publications.